survival book i

The Storm Within

chris j cole

Chris J. Cole (USA)
This edition published in 2021 by Chris J Cole (USA)
Copyright © Chris J Cole 2021
Cover Design © Sentinel Designs 2021
Cover Sword © Dreamstime
Editing Blazing Butterfly Edits 2021
Interior Format & Design © Sentinel Designs 2021

ACKNOWLEDGMENTS

I WOULD LIKE TO DEDICATE THIS BOOK TO A GOOD FRIEND WHO I CONSIDERED A BROTHER TO ME. WE LOST HIM TOO EARLY BUT I'VE COME TO REALIZE THAT HE LIVES IN ME NOW. TO ANTHONY OWENS AND HIS SON RICHARD. MISS YOU BOTH VERY MUCH. FLY HIGH

TO MY FAMILY, FRIENDS AND SUPPORTERS WHO MADE THIS POSSIBLE. I WOULDN'T HAVE BEEN ABLE TO PURSUE WHAT I LOVE IF IT WASN'T FOR YOU ALL PUSHING ME TO BE THE BEST I CAN BE.

IV

ONE

He was in the middle of a field, sword in hand, bodies littered on the ground around him. The crimson red sun reigned supreme in the blood-soaked sky. He was panting out of breath as the stench of blood filled his nose. Vultures swarmed the battlefield, swooping down from above to pick at the remains of the fallen. It did not matter who was friend or foe, for they were both food in the eyes of the ruthless scavengers.

He struck the ground beside him with his sword, falling to his knees. He could not catch his breath regardless of how many times he took in large gulps of air.

Then, from the depths of hell of an unknown origin, there was a terrible roar that erupted from all around him, making the miniscule hairs on his neck and spine stand on end. "Foolish boy," a cold voice said. "You really think you can defeat me? I've been around since the beginning of dawn. There's no way you can end me." There was a sound that sounded like laughter. "I, however, will have no problem ending you."

He got up to retrieve his sword before turning around and walking right into the teeth of a phantom creature.

Daniel jumped out of bed sweating profusely, his heart beating abnormally fast. He threw the blankets off of him and walked to the bathroom, running the water to let it get cold. He made a cup with his hands and ran them under the water, allowing them to fill up, then threw the water on his face to help him wake up. He breathed a sigh of relief; he was now fully awake and not shambling about anymore. Going back to his bedroom, he glanced at the clock on his bedside table. It read 6:40 AM in bold red numbers. *Might as well get ready for school,* he said to himself as he sat on one corner of his bed. He retrieved his headphones, plugged them into his phone and began playing some Five Finger Death Punch, nodding his head occasionally to the beat.

Twenty minutes later, he went downstairs to get something to eat. His father was sitting in his reclining chair listening to the news. He still could recur the dream he had, how it felt so real, like he was actually there but never knowing where there was. Of all the dreams he had had, no other had prolonged in his mind for this long. No other had affected him like this either; he had his head on a swivel, looking behind him at times to be safe. He was probably being paranoid but still…

He turned to watch the news as he waited for his mother to finish cooking. Nothing caught his interest. Out of his peripheral, he saw a black shadow coming to the side of him. He snapped his head to see his mother walking toward him with his plate.

He was sure she saw how wide eyed and anxious he was as she gently put her plate down, asking, "Are you alright? You look really antsy about something."

Daniel was in a cold sweat, his heart threatening to beat out of his chest. He wanted to tell her about the nightmare he had, but how would she respond? Would she just shrug it off and provide solace to him? He felt in his heart he should not tell her, the nightmare being too vivid for him to want to talk about it. He shook his head and proceeded to eat fast to avoid talking.

TWO

A surprise geometry test and a shocking conversation with his football coach telling him he had been cut from the team, made for a hellish day at school that he was looking to end. He sat on the bench waiting for his girlfriend, Mary. He lowered his head and tried to recollect himself for a moment, his stress and anger on the verge of being uncontrollable.

A pair of hands covered his eyes, followed by a whisper in his ear. "Guess who?"

Daniel smiled as he leaned his head back and kissed her. "How was your test, love?" he asked, all his anger boiling down to nothing now that she was here.

Mary snickered. "What test? I'm always ready for anything."

"You've always been smarter than me." He laughed to himself. "You have the highest GPA among our class so far, while I'm barely able to maintain a decent one at best. All I know is when we have kids, their brains are not going to be from me."

Mary smiled as she came around and sat next to him. "Do you remember how we met?"

Daniel had her hand in his tightly. "I try not to."

She slapped his arm with her free hand. Then, in a mimicky deep voice said, "I'll make it worth your while if you help me with my schoolwork. Please, I'm desperate."

Daniel laughed. "First off, I sound nothing like that. Second, you didn't seem to mind eating that big jar of jelly beans with me, did you?"

"How could I turn down free candy?"

Both of them laughed, Daniel put his hand over the small of her back and brought her in closer. "I got cut from the team today."

Mary's head snapped to his direction so fast he thought she had strained one of the muscles in her neck. "What? Why?"

"Coach said his star player was good to go. That he appreciated me contributing to the team, but they couldn't add me because of how many people could be on the team."

Daniel put his head down for a second until he felt Mary's finger lift his chin up. "Don't worry about him, then. That's more time for you to spend with me."

"Still," he said, looking down, "with everything I've been doing, I would have thought I'd have a bigger role and earned my place on the team. I spent so much time working on getting better."

"To hell with them. Football or no football, you are still loved and admired by those who love you. Like me." She jumped to her feet and grabbed both his hands. "Let's go out on a date night tonight. What do you say?"

"I say, what time?"

"Let's say, seven."

"You got yourself a deal."

Mary put her head against his and softly said, "I love you Daniel Smith. You better not be late."

They kissed, and as his lips touched Mary's, all his trouble seemed to have been erased. When they had broken away from each other, Daniel could see a couple of men in suits looking in his direction. *Who are they?*

"Who are they looking for?" Mary asked, turning to look at what Daniel was looking at.

Daniel shrugged. "I don't know, but I'm not about to stay here to find out."

Hand in hand they left the school grounds, walking down the street until they were out in front of Mary's house. "Let's put the day behind us," Mary said as they let each other go.

"What would I do without you?" Daniel asked with a smile on his face.

Mary followed that with a laugh of her own. "Goodness knows. You would probably be lost." She leaned in for one more kiss before walking up to her house.

Daniel waited until she had entered her house before reaching into his back pocket and taking out a small box. Inside it was a ring with a small diamond in the center. He smiled, thinking of what her reaction would be. He nodded to himself as he put the box back in his pocket. He would give it to her tonight during dinner. He continued walking, the troubles of his day gone, smiling both internally and on the outside.

Later that night, Daniel was sitting across the table from Mary waiting on their waiter. His heart was thumping loudly in his ears, sweat accumulating on his forehead. He was nervous; he was sure Mary could tell but she was either being too polite to say anything or she was nervous herself. Either way, the two of them sat there in silence.

Daniel cleared his throat while still fumbling with his fingers. "So, how long has it been since we had a date night?"

Mary took a sip of her water before responding. "Too long. And we've been together since freshman year."

"What did you like about me?" he asked, reaching for her hand.

She grabbed his and held his hand tightly. "Your smile. You always know what to say to make me feel better. There's quite a lot of your qualities that I admired and wanted to have myself."

"All to yourself? So selfish."

They both chuckled. "I can see a lot of good things coming your way Daniel. A lot of great things."

"Only with you by my side." He saw Mary's eyes begin to water. He continued, his heart open and vulnerable. "You know me better most times than I know myself. I feel myself wanting to spend the rest of my life with you. You're the only person I have become vulnerable with and I'm perfectly fine with that." He fell to one knee while getting the box out of his back pocket. "Mary, I'm tired of holding in my feelings toward you. When we graduate, I want to start our new chapter on the right note." He opened the box, revealing the diamond ring. Tears rapidly fell from Mary's eyes as she covered her mouth with her hands. "Will you promise to be mine forever and always, for as long as we both shall live?"

Mary wiped her tears with her napkin, the tears continuing to fall uncontrollably regardless. She sniffled a few times before nodding and saying, "I couldn't picture my life with anyone else. Yes, I promise!"

Daniel jumped to his feet and embraced her tightly, her head buried in his shoulders. He picked her up and kissed her for a full minute before setting her down and putting the ring on. Perfect fit.

She looked deeply in his eyes, a few stranded tears flowing freely. "I love you more than anything, Daniel Smith. I will always be your queen."

He smiled, his heart and mind content. "You better. You're stuck with me now."

They left the restaurant sometime later, never getting out of the grasp their hands were in. As they were leaving, Daniel felt the urge that someone was looking at him. When he looked behind him, he saw three men in suits eyeing them intently. He had a nasty feeling they were not here to make friends; he felt a strange vibe eminanting from them, yet he could not put his finger on what it was. His breathing became faster than normal, their eyes never wavered off one another until Mary asked, "Is everything okay?" She looked to where his eyes were and he knew she saw who he was looking at.

She turned back to face him and directed his head at her. "Don't worry about those clowns. Let's go home, love."

THREE

The next day, Daniel and Mary were practially inseparable. Except to go to their classes, they hung around the tables during their break. Mary admired her promise ring as the diamond glistened in the sun.

"You're so obsessed with that, aren't you?" Daniel asked Mary.

"You have no idea." She put her head on his shoulders. "I can't believe it; I'm so lucky I'm with you."

Daniel rested his head on top of hers, closing his eyes as he did so. The sun was out, casting a warm ray on him. "How was your class?"

She shrugged. "Not too bad. It's almost the end so I'm just embracing the suck."

It was lunchtime, which meant that most of the teachers and students were off campus, leaving a small portion of students wandering around. They would be back within the next hour; it was just enough time to clear their heads.

"Did you tell your parents about the ring?" Daniel asked Mary as the scent of her hair filled his nose.

Mary laughed. "My mom and dad noticed it as soon as I walked in the door. My mom complimented about how good it looked and my dad said it was about time."

"I think your dad will love me as a son."

"Oh yeah, no doubt. He likes you. If he didn't, you wouldn't still be with me."

Daniel smirked as he straighened himself up and opened his eyes. He gasped; there were four agents in front of him who were spread blocking his way out. He shrugged Mary off his shoulders, who was wide-eyed. They got off the bench, Daniel reaching for Mary's hand as his heart quickened. *Who are these guys? What do they want?*

"No time to think," Mary said under her breath. "We have to go. Now."

Mary snatched his hand and led the way down the hallway, pushing the guard who was in their way. She was surprisingly faster than usual and he was having a hard time keeping up with her. They ran until they came to the end of the hallway with classrooms going horizonatally down the hall. They tried to get into one of the classrooms, hoping it was open but it was to no avail. With nowhere left to run, they pressed their backs to the door as the four men in suits slowly approached; unfortunately for them, two more guards were coming from the left and right side, standing with their hands across, circling them in.

Daniel put his body in front of Mary, doing what he could to protect her. The men in suits still advanced, ever so slowly. "Who are you?" he asked angrily. "Why are you following us? What do you want?"

"So many questions," said a female disembodied voice from in front of him. Smoke formed in the middle of the circle the guards created and a moment later a woman appeared before them. She had long purple hair and from where he was he could see her bright, yellow eyes. "We just need to talk for a second."

"With eight men? Not the best way of saying you just want to talk," Daniel sneered

"If I were you, I wouldn't be worried about how many men I have, but I'd worry about who you are. That's what I want to know."

"He's not telling you anything!" Mary shouted from behind him. "So get lost!"

The mysterious woman laughed heartily. "Quiet little one, before something awful happens to you."

"What do you want from me?" Daniel asked, balling his hands into fists.

The mysterious woman took a step forward with her hand outstretched. "Come with me and let's get acquainted. Do this and your girlfriend lives. Don't, and she dies."

"I don't even know you, yet you expect me to just follow you?"

The woman shrugged, looking around before answering. "Yes. I mean if you want your woman to live. I would do as I was told." Daniel glanced at Mary, looking for answers. He could see that she was horrendously frightened, her eyes as wide as saucers. Beads of sweat ran down his forehead relentlessly, his body shaking. He didn't know what to do, let alone if he should follow through with it; looking at her and seeing her shake her head told him all he needed to know.

He turned his attention back to the woman and shook his head. "I'm not going anywhere with you or your goons."

The woman chuckled before pointing toward one of her men and gave him a nod.

The man in the suit stepped forward, pulled out his weapon and shot Mary once in the chest. Time seemed to have slowed down; Daniel stood there in shock as blood slowly began leaking out of her shirt, staining his hands.

He looked at the man who had shot her and growled. "What have you done?"

"Probably should have taken me up on my offer," the mysterious woman replied. "I'll be coming back. Make sure you make the right decision next time."

Daniel turned back to Mary and saw that the spot had only gotten bigger, his hand covered in blood. Her face was turning pale, her lips turning a shade of a light blue. There was nothing he could do, no matter how much he tried to apply pressure on the wound. Hot tears began streaming down his face; how could he have allowed this to happen? "Baby," he whispered, his voice quivering. "Baby, you gotta stay with me. Keep looking at me. Don't close your eyes."

Mary's breathing was extremely labored. She gazed into his eyes as she reached for his hand, grasping it tightly. "Anyone ever…tell y-you you're a h-hopeless romantic?" She smiled weakly.

"I love you. You can't go. You fight to stay awake, you hear me?"

Her cold hand brushed the side of his face. "It's too late for me. You stay strong. I—" She winced as she took a breath, her grasp getting a little loose. "It's too late for me."

Daniel's lower lip began shaking; he was trying to be strong for her but as he glanced at the promise ring that was now stained in her blood, his emotions overtook him. He laid his head on her bosom and listened to the faint beating of her heart. He could not hold back his tears anymore and weeped furiously, not concerned about the blood sticking to his skin. His heart felt like it was slowly ripping in two.

He looked into her still eyes, her chest no longer going up and down. Everything that gave his life meaning had been taken from him and shattered into a billion pieces. He closed her eyes before proceeding to take her promise ring from around her finger and putting it in her pocket. For one final time, he leaned in to kiss her forehead before pulling out his phone and calling an ambulance.

Daniel walked into his home and threw his backpack near the front door before running upstairs and slamming his bedroom door. He could not care less about anything school related, even life itself. His head ached as if a bowling ball had fallen on top of it, his eyes bright red and puffy. All he wanted to do, all he *cared* to do, was to mourn his girlfriend in peace, or at least attempt to.

There was a knock on the door, followed by his father saying, "You okay sport?"

Daniel ignored him, his face buried in his pillow. He didn't want to talk to anybody or hear anyone's voice; he just wanted to be in his own little world. *Who are those people in suits? Why are they after me? What's so special about me that they had to kill Mary?* His brain, despite the emotional state he was in, was buzzing with so many questions. *Is there more to my life than I think there is? Than what I have been living for almost eighteen years?* This time around, there was another knock on the door and then his mom's voice came shortly after. "Honey, could you please open up?"

Daniel groaned as he lifted himself from his bed and stumbled to the door. Her soft voice was full of concern; although he didn't want to open the door for anyone, he knew that she would be more comforting than his father. With his mother, he wouldn't feel awkward crying into her shoulder as he would feel with his dad, though he probably wouldn't tell him that. As soon as he turned the lock and opened the door, his mom flew in and embraced him tightly.

"You've always been more of a mama's boy since you were young," His mother laughed, looking down at her legs. "Pretty sure nine times out of ten if your father and I were side by side, you would still come to me. Why is that?"

Daniel shrugged, not knowing what to say. "Guess it's because you've always been just a tinge more understanding than him. I mean, I can go to him as well with no problem. It's just with these sensitive issues, I need more of a softer push."

His mother cleared her throat, looking down to see her fingers intertwined.

"Mary's parents got the call from the hospital shortly after they got there," his mother said as he tried to cover his bloodstained hands. "I am so sorry this happened to you, sweetheart. It tears me apart to see you like this." Without so much as a warning, she lunged toward him and embraced him tightly.

His body was still shaking from the trauma, getting tense even when his own mother touched him. He was in a state of shock, the realization of what happening not yet setting in for him. Slowly his hands reached around his mother's back to hug her back, his vision beginning to blur as he slowly managed to choke out the words, "Thanks mom."

"It's time you knew just why it happened."

Daniel pulled out of his mother's embrace with a puzzled expression on his face. "What do you mean?"

His mother closed her eyes, taking a deep breath in and slowly released it. This appeared to have been too hard for her to deal with. "This isn't easy for me. There is something that your father and I have not told you. We thought we could protect you, shield you from the horrors outside these four walls. Obviously we failed." She shook her head and got up. "You will find out soon enough. Get some rest. I'm sure Mary's parents are going to come here shortly and will want to know what happened."

"No!" Daniel protested. He stood up with a sudden fire in his eyes, his anger starting to boil over. "My girlfriend is dead! Whatever it is that I am, I need to know! You need to tell me what it was that it had to end with the death of my girlfriend and I need you to tell me now, before I find out for myself."

"It wouldn't make sense to you—" his mother started.

"Make it make sense."

His mother shook her head, this time more violently than before. "I'm sorry. I don't know how to say it without confusing you more.

Give me some time to get myself in order. I will give you the answers you seek, in time."

His mother left the room, closing the door behind her. The questions he had had before seemed to have multiplied tenfold within the confines of his mind. *Why won't my mother tell me what I am? What agenda do I need fulfill for that woman? Why did she need me to go with her to spare Mary's life?* He looked at his hands, seeing the lines running along his palm. *What is it that they find so special about me? I want to know.*

As he sat on his bed, he retrieved the picture on his bedframe, a picture of him and Mary wearing mouse ears. He smiled, his bottom lip quivering as he ran his finger over Mary's face. This particular picture was taken when their families had taken them to Disneyland during summer vacation. They deemed it their first date.

As his head hit the pillow, all he could manage to do was to look at her in that picture, reminiscing about what once was. This would be the only way he could remember her smile. He eventually went to sleep with the picture of his lost love on his chest.

FOUR

The room he was in was dark to human eyes, yet her vision allowed her to see it clear as day. To the left and right of where the man sat, were two large dogs that were two times bigger than an adult pitbull. From where she stood, she noticed his mouth latched on to a victim's neck as the victim screamed through a taped mouth. Even with her knowing the man, it sent shivers down her spine to the point where she had to look away. Seeing someone else feed was an uncomfortable feeling, especially when the victim was trying to writhe free like this victim was doing. She shook her head, remembering why she came. She bent a knee. "It's done, My Lord. I did what you wanted me to do."

He looked up, his bright red eyes igniting the darkness. He threw the woman down, wiping the corners of his mouth. "Are you sure? Was he the right one?"

"I am certain of it."

"You're certain of it?" The Lord stood up, hunched over as he made his way slowly to his chair in the middle of the room. "What do you mean, you're certain of it? Didn't I give you specific instructions to weed out the Chosen One?"

"Which I followed to a T, My Lord. His girlfriend was making it…

difficult…to do our job. We had to dispose of her.”

“What do you mean, dispose?”

“We had to kill her, My Lord.”

The Lord charged at her, slamming her against the wall, a deep growl resonating in his throat. “I gave you specific instructions to make sure that you got the right person, did I not?”

“You did, and he failed to come with me so we could question him further; we ended up taking who he cared about most. It had to be done.”

The Lord scoffed as he let go of her and went back to his chair. “He’s seen too much already. Dispose of him as well, whether he’s the Chosen One or not. He has seen too much.”

The woman put her eyes down. “Yes, My Lord.”

As she exited the cold, dark dungeon he was in, the Lord said one final thing that made her stop in her tracks. “And Penelope. Don’t fail me again.”

Penelope smirked as she turned around to face the Lord. “I wouldn’t dream of doing such a thing, Father.”

FIVE

Daniel snuck out of the house as soon as he woke up from his nap a couple of hours later. Retrieving his wallet and his Los Angeles Dodger military cap, he went downstairs as quietly as he could, unlocked the front door and gently closed it.

As he walked down the street with loud music coming in through his headphones, his eyes focused on the ground. When he came up to it, he couldn't help but stop at Mary's house. Her parents were at the foot of her house hugging friends and relatives as they did all they could do to help them cope with their loss.

Her mother wore a black dress and a veil to cover her eyes. She had a tissue at her disposal to wipe away the tears that decided to run down her cheeks. Her father was in a black suit embracing his wife while accepting hugs. From the distance, her dad were puffy eyed with dark markings underneath his eyelids. While their appearance was decent, he knew that both of them were a mess on the inside. as could be expected; the guilt that he felt quickly overwhelmed him and he had to keep going. He couldn't bring himself to approach them, let alone tell them it was his fault that their daughter was dead.

By the time he had reached into his pocket to mute his phone and removed his hoodie, he glanced up and saw the church bell towering above him some good fifty feet high. The windows were dark and tinted to block out the sun, the light brown texture of the building shining from the sunlight.

As he stepped into the church, it was barren; the pews were empty and each had enough *Holy Bibles* for anyone who might sit there. As he walked down the aisle to the cross in front of him that was in the center of the altar, it grew closer with each step. *In a week, I'm going to be carrying her casket. It all still feels like a dream.*

"It's been a while since you have set foot in this church, hasn't it?" somebody asked as they lit the candles on the right side of the altar. "Three years. If memory serves me right."

"I'm not big on religion," Daniel responded, taking a seat. "Not big on faith either to be honest."

"What brings you in?" the pastor asked, sitting next to him. "If not faith or your religion, something had to usher you in."

"Maybe I wanted to know when the service for my girlfriend is going to be. Other than that, you wouldn't find me here on any given Sunday."

The pastor looked disturbed at what he had just said. Finally, after a moment he said, "I am so very sorry for your loss. I know you and Mary were close but—"

"Everything happens for a reason. Right?" He held his composure, standing up and taking a few steps back, his eyes like daggers. "I've heard it all before pastor. If I didn't love my girlfriend, you would not see me for a very long time. That's what I think of your religion."

He walked towards the door but before he could push it open, the pastor called out after him. "One day you're going to have to choose the path you have been avoiding: the path to help those in need, or the path to condemn the whole world to an unforeseen mercy. Be careful and mindful of what you pick."

Daniel advanced out of the church, the warning going in one

ear and out the other. He sat on the third step leading down to the sidewalk. He looked at the clock on his phone, 2:35 PM. Almost the end of the school day. Something was telling him to go but at the same time, he didn't want to hear people's apologies or sympathetic words. *I'll just go back at five. When I know everybody will be at home.*

"Daniel," he heard a soft voice in front of him.

He knew immediately who it was and therefore he was reluctant to look up.

This time, the woman approached him and shook his shoulder for a second. "Daniel?"

"Yes?"

"What are you doing here?"

He took a moment before he responded. "Just wanted to get some fresh air."

"I'm happy that I found you here. I wanted to ask you something—"

He jumped to his feet and ran down the street, turning the corner and moving as far away from her as he could. He wasn't ready to tell her or to see the pain in her eyes. Not now anyway. The wound was still so fresh, in no way or form ready to heal. He sat down next to a big dumpster, put his headphones in, and tuned the whole world out, his head between his knees as fresh tears spilled out onto the ground.

Daniel woke up to drool on the side of his face and his playlist no longer playing. He took out his phone and realized it was a little after five o'clock. He also saw that he had a couple of missed calls from his parents followed by a few text messages. Now was the time to head to the high school and satisfy his hunger.

Half an hour later, he was at the front entrance of the school, the sun rapidly setting behind him. He would have to move fast to avoid being in the dark. He jogged down the darkened hallway to his locker, the sound of his footsteps echoing off the walls of the high school, the sweet smell of lemon pleasnatly filling his nostrils.

He reached Mary's locker, looked to both sides to make sure none of those agents or anyone else was coming his way before putting in her combination. When it had opened, he instantly went for her copy of the picture of them together in Mickey Mouse ears and the picture of them when they were little, around six. A piece of paper folded in a square caught the corner of his eye and, curious, he took it and put it in his pocket.

A deep, guttural growl resonated along the walls, sending waves of shivers down Daniel's spine. He didn't know where these sounds were coming from; they seemed to have been coming from all around him yet he couldn't pinpoint where. The hairs on both his arms stood on end, his pupils were dilated and he had a hard time trying to keep his breathing from shaking when his whole body compromised. He traversed down the hallway as slowly and steadily as he could, being careful so as not to have his footsteps be heard. With his tiptoing step, he looked around him to all sides, up and down and left and right, trying to listen for any sudden noise coming toward him.

When he got to the end of the hallway, he pressed himself up against the wall and closed his eyes, his chest rising and falling rapidly. He couldn't catch his breath. He closed his eyes, exhaled slowly, and dared himself to look. He got the courage to look down the hallway and was met with a mouthful of sharp teeth that grazed by his face. He stumbled to his feet as he glanced behind him to see the beast slide against the wall. He ran as fast as he could down the hallway into an empty classroom, slamming the door behind him and doing what he could to catch his breath. He pressed his hands against his mouth as the menacing growl grew louder and he could hear tapping sounds coming closer to him. He saw the shadow from under the door and closed his eyes, doing everything he could to keep his breathing down

"Your heartbeat is calm for a person who has two Hellhounds tracking you."

His feelings of mourning and grief turned instantaneously to that of anger and revenge. He knew who it was and he wanted nothing more than to rip her throat out. He didn't care what these *Hellhounds* were, or what they were capable of doing. He came out of his hiding spot and put his hands up, ready to fight.

From the shadows glowed two more red eyes. "Do you know what I am, Daniel Gates? I do not play nice but most of all, I do not fight with my knuckles!" A blue light shot at him; with a half second to react, he ducked down and avoided the blast. *What the hell?* He scrambled to his feet.

"What are you?" His anger threatened to overtake him.

The shadowy woman laughed, the Hellhounds at her feet, waiting to be told otherwise. "More powerful than you. Are you ready to die?"

"Not before I take you with me!"

As he began running towards her, he was blinded by a bright white light. He threw his hands up to shield his eyes and could feel his body lift up in the air. When the light died down, he had to adjust to the new surrounding that was his home. He rubbed his eyes and noticed his parents in front of him and when he turned behind him, he noticed a muscular man with shoulder long brown hair standing over him.

"What happened?" Daniel asked, letting his eyes adjust to the different light. Someone was trying to help him to his feet but he slapped their hand away, even though he was barely able to stand on his feet alone.

He was still shaking from the encounter with the hellhounds, as well as the encounter with the mysterious woman. On top of that, he was confused about who these two people were and what they wanted. He sat on the couch and got his bearings together, the adrenaline working overtime as his body was shaking furiously from head to toe.

"You almost sealed your fate," the man behind him said, eyeing him closely. "Going up against a vampire is one of the most stupidest deaths in the history of mankind."

"I'm sorry, but who are you?" Daniel asked, his fists balled up and ready for action. "Who's the vampire? Why are they after me? Why are you guys here?" He took a step closer to the tall man eyeing him. "Who are *you?*"

The man looked down at his fists and smiled, each smelling the other's breath. "If you think you're fast enough to land that first punch, do it tough guy."

Daniel's dad appeared in the living room, a man with a bald head stood next to him. "Balisnor. Daniel," he said both their names sternly but none fidgeted, not even an inch. They stayed in place, staring persistently, intently, until the bald man took his turn. "Balisnor! Show some restraint!"

The man named Balisnor broke his eye contact with Daniel, though he was reluctant, and stepped back a few paces.

"Please sit," the bald man stated with a smile on his face. When Daniel did, he went on. "My name is Erek. You have already met my bodyguard Balisnor. First off, I want to offer my deepest condolences to you for your loss. I know it's not easy but trust me when I say, things get better."

Daniel looked at his dad and didn't hide how he was feeling when he opened his mouth. "How much did you pay this therapist? Because now would be a perfect time to get your money back."

"Don't be rude to our guest Daniel. He's not a therapist. He comes far and wide to explain what we cannot. Your mother and I love you and want the best for you but we can't hide the truth from you any longer."

"What is it that you and mom can't tell me? Am I adopted?"

Erek was the one who answered this time. "If you want me to be honest with you, these folks you refer to as your mom and dad are not your actual parents. They were assigned to protect you and, up until this point, they have done a spectacular job. However, in this unfortunate scenario, it is no longer safe for you."

Daniel's mind was now whirring. *If these people are not my parents, then where the hell are my real ones? And what did Erek mean when he said it was no longer safe? Why am I no longer safe? What is going on?*"I'm confused. Why is it no longer safe?"

"It's too much to explain. We don't have time to break down everything you want to know. That vampire is going to stop at nothing until she has you in her possession."

"How do you expect me to help you when I don't even know who I am, or what my calling is?"

Erek took a step toward him. "We can help you find your calling but you would need to come with us, which means you would have to leave everything you have come to know behind. All those stories about vampires, elves, dwarves, all those mythological creatures that live rent free in your mind," he chuckled to himself, "they're all real. You're more important than you think. Let us help you in releasing your full potential."

"I'm not going anywhere until I go to my girlfriend's funeral. Your movement can shrivel up and die before I turn my back on her and go somewhere with complete strangers."

Balisnor and Erek open their mouths to speak before his father figure raised a hand and chimed in. "Let me talk to you in private for a second."

He and Daniel got up and proceeded to go to the kitchen, out of prying ears and sharp dagger eyes. "You're making this impossible Daniel. And at the wrong time. She will be coming here next."

"My life has been a lie!" Daniel said through gritted teeth. "I don't know who the hell is who anymore. My real parents are somewhere else and the people I thought were my parents are decoys instead. When were you going to tell me?"

His father's head slumped down in shame. "I'm sorry. I thought this would never happen. We would have told you, but we never saw a reason to. It's our fault that time has run out for you to know who you truly are meant to be. There comes a time when we must all make a decision that will make an impact in our lives. You must make one." His father patted his shoulder, trying to be reassuring.

Daniel was livid, and it showed clearly in his face. "What about Mary's funeral? You want me to just forget about her?"

"It's never easy making a decision out of a complex situation like this one." He shrugged. "However, to answer your question, yes."

Daniel couldn't bring himself to make such a fast decision in such a short time. *How do I put my life into the hands of two people I have never met? How do I go with them knowing that I won't be able to tell Mary goodbye one final time? I can't! This is just plain stupid to go along with!* However, he knew there had to have been some truth behind some of what was said.

The vampire lady they mentioned would hunt him until he was found, which meant that he risked getting those he loved getting in harm's way. He couldn't allow that. He sighed deeply and asked Erek, "Would I be able to come back here?"

Erek smiled reassuringly as he walked into the room. "Yes, but right now your vampire lady will stop at nothing until her hunt is complete. With Balisnor and I, you are safer there than here; I can promise you that."

"And should I fail at coming with you?"

"Then the world you know and love will be in infinite darkness. Trust me Daniel. You need us more than we need you."

Balisnor snorted loudly enough for Daniel to hear. "Isn't that the truth?"

His dad had a gleam in his eye, putting a hand on his shoulder. "It's going to be hard, transitioning from one life to another. However, you won't have to be at a disadvantage when enemies come for you. If we are destined to meet again, then may the goodness of the earth make it so. If not, I wish you nothing but the best."

"You just expect me to throw away the life I have come to know? Just because? This is my family we're talking about me leaving behind to fend for themselves! You can't expect me to be good with this! You just can't!"

"Listen, you little runt," Balisnor said. "What's going on is bigger than you; it's bigger than me. It's bigger than even your family. Now you're going to come with us even if it means we drag you."

"Not me," Erek intervened, putting his hands in the air.

"I will. And very happily, I won't lie."

Daniel's knuckles were white as snow. He didn't like Balisnor one bit and wanted nothing more than to get one good punch in. He looked in the direction of his dad, who nodded and smirked. He looked at Erek and reluctantly nodded his head. "Fine. I'll go with you but it's not because I want to. Or because I care about your little revolt. I'm going so I can keep my family safe."

"And that's a good enough answer for me dear boy." Erek put his arm around his shoulder and escorted him to the living room where his parents sat.

With a deep breath, he looked at his parents and said, "I've decided to go with them. Not because I want to, or because I give a damn about what I mean to them," he looked at Balisnor and said to his face, "because I don't. I'm going so that you're not in danger anymore."

His dad got up and embraced him, followed shortly by his mother. "We are so proud of you for making the right choice. It's not the end there bud. Trust in these people. You might come to like the place."

"Yeah, well, we'll see. I love you guys. Thank you for everything you've done for me." He looked at Erek and gave him the affirming nod. "Let's go, before I change my mind."

Erek got up with a bright smile on his face. "Excellent! And of course, of course! We should go now, before it's too late."

Daniel trudged over to them and waited, not wanting to make eye contact with Erek or Balisnor. He looked at his parents, however, and managed to smile. "May we meet again."

"You will find the answers you seek," his mother said, smiling reassuringly.

"We will meet again," his father stated as he watched Daniel vanish before their eyes. "Stay strong," he whispered.

SIX

The last thing Daniel saw before it turned to a white nothingness was his parents waving goodbye. He felt empty, like he was saying goodbye to his old life as well as his family. It was like a deep void that he now had, and he wasn't too sure of how to fill it. The thought of having to start a new life in a new land was a little overwhelming for him to consider knowing that the situation that he was in. He teared up a bit, anxiety in his heart over how long it would take before he saw his family again. After twenty seconds of free falling, his feet finally hit the ground…then his knees. "Ow," he grunted as he got up and dusted off. His mood instantly turned sour when he saw that Balisnor and Erek were still on their feet. He could have sworn that Balisnor had a smirk on his face.

From where they landed, all that was in his field of vision were tall majestic trees that towered above him like skyscrapers. Their thick trunks were enough to house a family of three, their luscious leaves and thick branches blocking out the sun completely, making for plenty of shade. Birds sang from atop these trees, butterflies dancing as the cool wind kissed his skin. The fresh air filled his nose, taking him by surprise over how clean it was.

"Varin is not much to look at," Erek said as they made their trek through the trees, leaves crunching beneath their feet. "If you go too far into the woods, however, there will be things that will be the stuff of nightmares."

"Like what?" Daniel asked as he looked around him. "Where are the mosquitoes? The poison ivy? This place is too perfect if you say there isn't any of that."

Erek looked confused. "What are mosquitoes and this poison ivy you speak of? There is no such thing as these."

"Get out of here," Daniel replied with a smile on his face. "Maybe this place isn't too bad. Definitely something I can get used to."

"I thought you said you couldn't care less about why you're here," Balisnor chimed in, his position to the right of Daniel.

"Don't think I was talking to you, so butt out of the conversation, would you?"

Balisnor chuckled to himself. "You have no idea what you're in for. Just wait kid. I got you and your mouth."

They passed the treeline ten minutes later and the scenery just got better. Daniel was so taken aback by the beauty of this alien place that he had to stop and observe it for a full minute before catching up with Erek and Balisnor.

To the immediate right of the treeline was a big lake; behind that were snow-capped mountains that made a bowl around them. It was unlike anything he had ever seen. *Maybe I won't have a hard time finding my calling here after all.*

Up ahead was a large, marble castle. On both sides were large watchtowers with a small square window overlooking the forest behind him. The main castle was made of the purest form of marble and had numerous windows gutted inside it. It must have been at least eight stories. At the very top of the castle were large windows that, on the inside, probably stretched from the floor to the ceiling. He suspected that was where the royal family resided. Behind the castle were tall, snow capped mountains illluminating the majestic landscaape before him. The majestic building was protected by a thirty-foot high brick wall that blocked what looked to be more smaller buildings going toward the castle, but with the wall erected and the door presently closed, he couldn't be certain as to what else was in there. Soldiers with white armor and blue-haired mohawk on their helmet made it impossible to see their faces up close. He watched as they patrolled the area. He assumed they were soldiers, as they wore the same color chestplate, some of them carrying swords while at the very top of the wall were a line of soldiers with bows. All of them had a white helmet on, a silhouette of an eagle in the center of their chestplate.

"Where are we?" Daniel asked, not able to take his eyes off the beautiful scenery before him.

Erek smiled, putting his hand on Daniel's shoulder. "The castle before you houses the most powerful royal family within the Five Kingdoms. This one is called Varin. Welcome to your new home."

SEVEN

When they approached the wall sometime later, there were guards waiting for them. "Your Majesty," one of the guards said as he stepped aside and allowed them to pass.

They walked along the cobblestone roads, little shops lined up along the sides of it. There were little canopies constructed out front to protect their products from any elements that might come their way. Everywhere he looked, he saw these people smiling behind the tables, watching them as they walked past.

The cobblestone street under his feet suddenly turned to solid marble. When he glanced up, he noticed he was in the hallway leading to the castle. As they made their way up the stairs, he noticed lanterns lined along the walls, none of which were lit due to the time of day. Overhead was an enormous crystal chandelier that hung in the middle of the room. Torches lined the walls every ten or so feet. Still, they kept walking.

Finally, after a measly two minutes, they came across two giant, double wooden doors that stood at least thirty feet high. They creaked as they opened, revealing a magnificent room behind them. The room was massive enough to fit the whole Kingdom into it, if need be. The walls on all four sides were white, with a large dome-shaped glass overhead so they could see whatever elements afftected Varinians that day, whether it was rain, thunderstorms, or snow. Today's weather was sunny. There were no clouds in sight; the rays poured through the dome, making it that much brigher in the hall. When they had walked through and stepped into the room, Daniel gasped at the beauty.

The throne room had a sunroof, allowing the sunlight to pour in and make the room appear golden. At the end of the room was a stage where three thrones rested in the middle. The thrones were made of the same marble the castle was constructed out of.

"Welcome to the most magnificient kingdom among the Five Kingdoms. This is the throne room. Isn't it magnificent? Come meet my wife."

Standing in front of either side of the middle throne were two women. The woman on the right had to be his wife due to the fact she looked to have been in her mid to late twenties. She had long platinum blonde hair that was braided from just above her ears and had piercing but stunning emerald green eyes. She wore a simple yet elegant headband that had rhinestones all along through it; in the middle, it was shaped like a small "**v**." She had a bright, welcoming smile on her face but for some reason, Daniel felt like it was just for show, like her true colors would come out once he got to know her.

The girl next to her was far younger, looking Daniel up and down before making eye contact. She smiled at him, as if intrigued by his presence. She wore a blue dress that hugged her curves rather tightly. Her long, jet black hair fell on her back, Her deep blue eyes locked onto Daniel's that it felt like he couldn't move. She was hypnotizing him, and he liked it.

On her head was a jeweled crown that had a variation of precious stones; strapped to her waist were two sharp sai, the hilt sporting a circular ruby.

Erek joined them and hugged them at the same time before turning to face Daniel. "This is my kingdom. From this point forward, you are a Varinian, which means you will follow our customs and courtesies and face the same punishment as the people born here do. This is my wife, your Queen, Guinevere, and my daughter, your Princess, Anya." Daniel bowed his head in Anya's direction but she kept looking at him with that cold dark stare, making him feel uneasy.

The king continued, "You will start training tomorrow. The sooner you are taught to defend yourself from those that are after you, the sooner you are able to return home with no fear. Go. Explore your new home. Anya here will be your escort."

Princess Anya smirked, not once breaking the eye contact set between them. "Very well." As she made her way down the stairs, she walked by him and whispered, "Looking forward to it."

EIGHT

Mr. Gates's face was covered in blood. Three claw marks, no less than an inch thick, marred his face. His wife sat across from him, crying, her make-up leaving trails of black down her face.

Penelope, amidst the tears and screams as well as the blood spatters on the walls, was smiling, her long claws stained with bright red. "Is he the Chosen One?" she asked for the umpteenth time. "Tell me and I'll stop. Don't," she thrust her fingers into his thigh, smiling and laughing with her mouth open as his screams filled her ears, "and I keep going."

"I don't know!" Mrs. Gates screamed at the top of her lungs, her teeth gritted, and her face stained with tears. "What did you expect him to do when he watched you kill his girlfriend? He's scared, so of course he's going to hide."

Penelope tilted her head in her direction, her claws still digging into Mr. Gates' leg. After a long minute, she pulled up and extracted her claws from his flesh. She slowly walked to the other side where his wife was and stroked her finger down her cheek in a slow motion. She got so uncomfortably close to her face that Mrs. Gates could hear her excited breaths. "It wasn't that hard, now was it?"

Mrs. Gates shook her head, her breaths trembling.

"But I'm afraid what you said is not going to work. You see, I need a pinpoint location as to where he is."

"I told you, I don't know where he is. I'm telling you the truth."

"Are you though?" She straightened herself and stood in between them. "I grow bored. So, if you cannot give me the information I need, then you are of no use to me."

The room got quiet. Neither of them talked, causing Penelope to roll her eyes. "Very well." She walked to Mr. Gates with her claws out and stabbed him through his heart, sticking through his back. "The next time I ask you a question, answer it to the best of your ability."

Mrs. Gates screamed as she saw her husband's life ebb away. "I'm sorry," she whispered as she let the tears flow. "I'm so sorry, my love."

Penelope bent down with her sick smile still intact. "His blood is on your hands. Tell Daniel the Dark King is going to be looking for him for the rest of his days. Tell him there's no place he can hide that he will be safe." A second later, Penelope was gone and Mrs. Gates was still tied to the chair, her husband already dead.

NINE

Once he had been shown around the castle, the King and two of his guards showed him to his room. A single candle was ablaze on top of a tall dresser, the sun pouring in through a big window. He stepped in and saw that the wooden floors didn't creak as he slowly advanced into his room, unsure if this was supposed to be a trap or not. He went over to the window and looked at the scenery before him, which was of the magnificent forest he had come to admire. The trees swayed slowly in the calm wind, going this way and that way ever so gracefully. He watched blue jays and cardinals flying around nonchalantly, without a care in the world.

He turned to the King, who was smiling as he crossed his arms. "Is this a trap?"

King Erek laughed, dropping his arms and walking towards him. "Visitor or not, our guests get the best. Rest up, because tomorrow you start your training."

"Yes sir," Daniel said, bowing his head.

Erek leaned in and whispered in his ear. "Remember, it's Your Majesty. Don't worry. It takes some time transitioning."

Daniel cleared his throat before saying, "Yes, Your Majesty."

As the king was leaving, his daughter appeared at the entrance and smiled at her father. When the King nodded his head in acknowledgment, she returned the gesture. "May I enter?"

"Yes, Your Majesty." He was confused as to what to say or do. Part of him was telling him to bow; the other was telling him not to make a fool out of himself and instead wait to be told. *What do I do?*

The princess smiled widely, taking a step closer. "You don't have to do that with me. I'm your princess, nothing more or less than that. When we're out in public however, just address me as Your Highness."

"Yes…Your Highness." His heart began to thump as she smiled, taking another step closer to him. He felt a tingle in his body that flooded through him, a sensation he had never felt before, not even with…

"How are you liking Varin?" the princess asked as she sat on his bed.

Daniel tried not making eye contact. *Why is she in my room? Still, just play along.* He looked down at the floor as he moved past her. "I…I'm liking it…so far."

"If you like what's inside the walls, you're going to love the outside. It's beautiful, majestic, exuberant. Too many words come to my head when I think about it." The princess got up and walked over to the window, letting out a sigh. Her silver crown glistened in the sun's beams as it rays shone through the window. The jeweled prongs that jutted out from the curve twinkled in its light.

"You'll have to show me one day," Daniel said with an awkward smile, staying rooted to where he was at.

Princess Anya stood up and stood so close to him, he could smell the wild strawberry scent of her hair. "I keep my promises, Daniel

Gates. Complete your training and I promise to take you out beyond the wall."

"How do I know you're not saying that to trick me? With all due respect Princess, I don't know you. I have never met you a day in my life. Why should I take your word for it?" Daniel wanted to trust her, but he was hesitant. He didn't know if he should or not, and it was making him upset. There was a knock on the door and they broke apart quickly. It was Balisnor who had walked in on them. Daniel's anger took its natural course at the sight of the Chief Bodyguard. They eyed each other menacingly for a brief moment before Balisnor turned to the Princess and asked, "My Lady, are you alright?"

The princess fixed herself up and smoothed out her dress. "I'm fine Balisnor, thank you. I was just telling him good luck with his training tomorrow."

Daniel went over to his table where his pitcher of water was and poured himself a glass, choosing to be oblivious to their conversation simply for the sheer fact not to hear Balisnor's voice. It was toward the end of their talk that he decided to hear what was being said.

"Your father would like to see you, My Lady, hence why I'm here."

"Very well." She looked Daniel in the eye once more and whispered, "Good luck. I will be watching."

"Yes, Your Highness."

When she had left and was out of earshot, Balisnor walked in and said, "You start training tomorrow. You need to focus and get out of your head anything that may hinder your performance. Can you do that for me?"

"Yes sir."

Daniel couldn't help but think about the obvious. To be asked to put that in the back of his head and focus solely on this training Balisnor spoke of, was hard for him to do. Yet he knew he had to try not for his sake, or even the Princess, but for his family. Well, his decoy family. He balled up his fists and tried to recollect himself as a swarm of emotions ran his way, trying to take turns in torturing him. Balisnor, in seeing the torment in his student's eyes, said, "I know what troubles you, but you need to know they made the right decision in bringing you here."

How does he know what troubles me? He hasn't walked in my shoes! He doesn't know the pain of hearing that the family he grew up with since he was a toddler isn't actually his family! What does he know about pain? Loss? Not being able to find your identity and where you stand in this world?

He bottled this raw anger and took a deep breath before replying to Balisnor. "That's not what I'm upset about Balisnor. It's the fact that my real parents just might be here and I don't have a fathom of an idea where to start looking. Of where I can get the answers to the questions that haunt me day in and day out since finding out the family I once knew, isn't my real mother or father. So, the sooner we start and I learn what you want me to learn, the sooner I can get out of these walls and seek what's been awaiting me all this time."

"Make a name for yourself and I promise you, they will hear about you and come. Put all that worry to rest and show us what you got."

He smiled and, in return, Daniel smiled back. "Yes sir."

Balisnor went to the door, then turned around as if he had forgotten something. "I suggest you keep your relationship with the princess secretive. You have a lot to show Erek before he even *allows* you to be with her alone. Keep it professional when out and about. What you two do behind closed doors is none of my business."

Daniel nodded to Balisnor to let him know he understood before the big guy made his way out, leaving Daniel to his lonesome. He dug in his pocket and retrieved a square piece of parchment. When he had opened it, his eyes filled with tears as they set upon a picture of Mary and him smiling widely for the camera, cheek to cheek.

Almost immediately, both depression and grief set in, bringing him into that dark atmosphere he thought he had ridden himself of. The same picture he had retrieved from her locker was the same that he held here and now. He wiped his eyes as that warm smile touched him once more. "I miss you," he said to her, his hands shaking. "I don't know how I keep pushing myself to go on. Some days are worse than others." His lip quivered as he dug out the ring. "You remember this? How happy you were? How happy *we* were? I wish I could join you, so we could be together again. This pain is just too much for me to take. I know you would want me to keep going. I get it. I just need to feel you again, to talk with you just one last time." He lay on his bed with his hands outstretched and examined it until his eyes grew heavy and he couldn't stay awake no longer. When he had felt the urge to sleep, he took off his shoes and placed the picture next to his bed before getting in the covers and dozing off. *I love you, Mary.*

TEN

After forty-eight hours since being tasked with her current mission, it seemed she had finally become familiar with the dark room her father had inhabited with her. Her superb vision could pick out the tiles that were stained with human blood from the various places her father had fed. It was a spacious room, with no windows and a couple of AC vents to make it cold and favorable for his…condition. This was the place she stayed until her father decided to send her out again; so, in the meantime, she stayed up in the ceiling on top of one of the rafters, observing this space that her and her siblings called home.

"Perhaps I should put someone who's a bit more competent on your mission since the taste of failure is on your lips," his cold voice echoed off the stone walls. "I would do it myself but…" There was a sigh from the shadows. "My current state will not allow it."

"Father," Penelope said, doing her best to look at the floor instead of looking at where the throne was, which she knew he would take as a challenge. "I have done everything you have set me out to do and have not been wrong." She took a deep breath to steady herself. "Yet."

Mortezan was silent for a moment, then uttered, "Go on."

Penelope growled. *How am I supposed to persuade him when he doesn't believe I'm doing my best now? It doesn't make sense.* She knew if her reasoning wasn't what he wanted to hear, she would lose his confidence in her. She wanted to prove to her father she could do this on her own. She had to. "I know for a fact he's in Varin, Father. Let me take a few of my hounds and I won't come back until I have his head."

Her father was quiet until he said a few seconds later, "Very well. If he is there, you will lead my army to their front gate. If not, I will relieve you of this task and you will be exiled for all eternity. Do we have an agreement?"

"Yes, My Lord."

She let out a shrill whistle as she jumped down from her space and landed between two of her hounds, who growled lowly at the sudden movement. With now a few by her side by tapping her thigh, she took off with a pep in her step. She surely missed Varin; but she wouldn't mind it burning to the ground.

ELEVEN

Princess Anya sat on her chair, humming to herself as her maid combed her hair. She was lost in her thoughts; more clearly, she was lost in her thoughts pertaining to Daniel. There was a certain trait that she was attracted to. Maybe it was because he was new; or perhaps she could had some sixth sense that told her he was the one. All she knew was that it felt as if they were carrying different magnets of the opposite charge and when he had come through that wall, it was something immediate that happened. She laughed to herself as the word came back around to the center of her mind. Attracted. *He hasn't been here a whole day and I'm attracted to an outsider. How does that make sense?* She snapped back to her senses as she heard a voice ask, "Is everything alright, My Lady?"

"Hmm?" The princess jumped up and, when she realized that it was her maid, she shook her head and smiled. A look of concern came from her ocean blue eyes, her blonde hair in a ponytail as she held the brush against the princess' head. "Yes, yes of course. Just got something on my mind."

"Something, or someone?"

Princess Anya gazed into the mirror to see her maid smirking as she kept brushing her hair at a slow pace, not seeming to be in a rush.

The princess smirked. "Maybe it's a bit of both." *Is it that obvious? If my maid can see it, can my parents see it as well?*

The maid stepped to the side of the princess with her mouth agape. "You must tell me more about this lucky person."

Princess Anya shifted to face the maid and smiled widely. "He's from the human realm and just arrived in Varin today." She put her hand up to stop Dana from brushing, getting to her feet as she combed her hair with her fingers.

"Go on My Lady." Dana put the brush down and faced her princess with a smile on her face. "What is it that you like about him?"

"I don't know what it was about him, but I felt a connection to him. Like we were supposed to be with each other." She put her hand up just in time to stop her maid from talking. "It can't happen I know, but still…there's something about him that makes me feel things I have never felt before. ."

"Be careful, My Lady. You don't want to upset your father. Goodness knows what he would do if he was to find out."

You don't think I know that? The princess looked annoyed, knowing what would happen if this was to reach outside ears. She was nervous about telling her maid, her closest friend since she was little. "Which is why you must not tell a soul about it. I mean it, Dana."

"I won't," the maid said as she smiled widely once more. "You can be rest assured your little secret is safe with me."

"Thank you." Princess Anya yawned, putting her hands in the air as she did so. "I have to be awake early tomorrow so I'm afraid I'm going to be retiring for the night Dana." She proceeded to walk to her bed and pulled back on the blankets just enough for her to get in.

Dana curtsied to her Princess, the smirk never fading from her face. "Yes, My Lady. See you in the morning."

With Dana now gone and the princess in her bed, she stayed awake for a moment trying to find out just why she felt so connected for a stranger that she had just met today. *Is it destiny finally coming my way after all these years? Meant to be? I must be insane. To have feelings for an outsider is forbidden. If the other four Kings found out, it would spell disaster for my people. Chasing my heart, chasing my desire, it can't be that bad...can it?* She did not know, but what she did know was that she had to get to the bottom of it fast. She dozed off, drifting into a deep sleep and thinking about it no more.

TWELVE

Daniel woke the next day to the sound of someone rambunctiously knocking on his door. Groggy and feeling heavy lidded from not sleeping well, he got out of his bed and walked slowly to the door with his head down. His eyes felt like they weighed a good ten pounds, making it difficult to keep them open. He threw the covers off him and made his way to the door. A soldier greeted him on the other side and he knew that today really was here. Today was his first day of training.

"Balisnor is waiting for you at the ground sir," the soldier said. "Get ready and follow me so we can be on our way."

Daniel nodded as he shut the door and got ready. He noticed the clothes on the foot of his bed. *I don't know how they did it, but I won't complain.* He decided to walk to the closet. Once opened, he realized they had supplied him with ten sets of clothes to help him blend in with the rest. He took out a set and put them on the bed, putting on the pants first before anything else.

After twenty minutes of almost falling on his face because his pants kept getting stuck, he finally made it out to explore inside the wall just a bit more. As he took the last step down from the stairs, he made his way to a couple of shops right outside. The first one he went to had baskets of various fruits such as apples, bananas, oranges, and mangoes. He looked at the owner of the stand, who smiled a toothless smile and bowed his head, motioning for him to take one. Daniel got an orange and shook his head. "I don't have anything to give you."

The man's voice was raspy as he replied, "Don't worry about it, good sir. Consider it on the house."

Daniel bowed his head in return and went to the next shop to see that there were different types of fish in large pans. From salmon filets to whole tuna sitting on ice, there were plenty of them to choose from. Daniel nodded his head and smiled at the owner, leaving with just his orange. *I got to come back here. It's like a little Farmer's Market.* As he walked toward the training grounds to meet Balisnor, he ripped into his orange and enjoyed the sweet, juicy and succulent taste of its flesh. As the sun spilled over the peak of the mountains, a blend of purple and orange hues painted the sky like a canvas. He crossed his arms to stop his body from shivering as the chilled air froze him to his bones and the even colder breeze kissed his face softly.

"It's not bad once you get used to it," the soldier said from beside him. "You think it's cold now? Wait until the snow hits here in a couple of weeks. You'll be in trouble then Mr. Shivers."

The guard ushered Daniel to follow him, leading the way down the trail that started from the beginning of the shops all the way around the side of the castle. All that was there were windows to signify how many floors the castle had, which were six floors in total. They walked for an extra five minutes before coming to the training grounds, where Balisnor, the King, and Princess Anya were waiting.

"Morning," Balisnor boomed when they had reached him. The guards broke off and went on their merry way, leaving Daniel in Balisnor's care. "How are you feeling today?"

"Nervous. Anxious. I don't know," Daniel replied, feeling as if he had given Balisnor an honest response. He had a million and one emotions flooding him at once that he suddenly felt nauseous.

Balisnor laughed as he placed his hand on his shoulder. "Don't worry. I'll take it easy on you for your first day."

Daniel nodded, the nerves shaking him awake and making him jittery instead. Whether it was the cold or not, he wasn't sure; his hands started shaking, the adrenaline flowing richly through his body.

"Right. So, uh, let's get started." Balisnor led Daniel to the training ground. He tossed a wooden sword Daniel's way. Once he had picked it up from the ground, Balisnor rushed and swept his leg, causing him to land on his back. "Lesson one, be prepared."

Daniel got up and held the sword with both his hands, the wetness of his shirt soaking to his back. This time, he was the one to rush Balisnor, but he got his sword whacked from his hand and Balisnor's weapon was quick to slash against the back of his leg. Had it been a real sword, it would have shredded ligaments and tendons, rendering the leg completely useless. Thankfully, they were wooden and didn't have any damage.

"Lesson two. Never rush your opponent. You want to study him, get to him mentally. If you get in his head successfully, that's half the battle that you've already won."

He got to his feet again, retrieved the sword once more, and waited patiently, doing his best to read what Balisnor would possibly do. After a minute of no advancement towards one another, he felt a sharp pain erupt from the base of his neck. He turned around and saw that one of the guards was the culprit who had done it. "And lesson number three," Balisnor said from behind. Daniel rolled his eyes and didn't bother turning around. A second later, he was thrown from Balisnor's back and he landed on his side, making him lose wind for a minute. "Never expect a fair fight." He extended his hand, helping Daniel to his feet and dusting off his shoulders.

Throughout the course of the day, as the sun rose to its highest in the sky, Balisnor taught Daniel the different techniques of wielding a sword; how to parry, dodge, work on his stance. Every time Daniel got it wrong, Balisnor would make him pay by slapping him wherever was free, whether it was on his calf or shoulder. Daniel fought on, doing everything he could to push on until his calf was bruised, making it hard for him to stay on his feet on his own. He limped off the training ground and sat on the grass, wincing in pain as it took control of his body. *Well, I'm no longer cold.* He looked up at the sky and saw that the sun was at the highest part, sweat soaking on his shirt.

Balisnor looked at Daniel with pity in his eyes and said, "I think that's enough for today."

He saw the princess looking from the side and rage filled him. Rage that he was being humiliated in front of her, in front of people he never seen before. He put down his sword and said, "I'm done."

Balisnor nodded. "Indeed. Time to get some rest. We'll pick it up tomorrow. Guard, show him to his chambers."

That night, Daniel layz on his bed, his body sore from the so-called training Balisnor had put him through today. He was pondering his life choices, debating whether staying was really worth the humiliation.

A soft tap on the door woke his senses as he lazily made his way to the door to find the princess waiting for him. "My Lady," Daniel mumbled as he stood with the door ajar.

"Thought you would enjoy the company," she said almost in a whisper, a smile on her face to try to cheer him up. "Let me in. Please."

Reluctant but not wanting to anger her, he stepped aside and let her pass by, her hair smelling like freshly ripe strawberries and honey. still managed to get him tingly inside.

She sat down at the foot of his bed and placed her hands on her legs. "I know it can be difficult to adapt to how we operate. It will be all worth it though, when your training is done and you're officially one of us."

"With all due respect My Lady, I don't know if I can ever be what you expect me to be. I still haven't found who I am, or am supposed to be. At this rate, I'm wasting my time and yours, and you know that. I don't know how many times I've had to tell you I'm not here on my own accord. I'm here so my scent or however this vampire is tracking me doesn't hurt my…" He stopped himself, forgetting that what he was saying wasn't exactly true. He looked down, sighing heavily as he did so. "I don't know if I can be what you think I can in the time I have. It's impossible Princess. I'm sorry."

The princess stood up and walked next to him, putting her hand to his heart. His cheeks turned a rosy red knowing that she could feel his heartbeat quicken, as if it would explode out of his chest at any moment. "You need to look deep within yourself and find what you are made of.

"If you need me to do this, I need to see my family. See how they're doing. That's all I'm asking." He backed away, his heart rate returning to normal. "If not, then I'm afraid I can't help you."

Daniel watched the Princess turn around to stare out the window. Finally, after a minute or so, she said, "I'm not supposed to do this because it can be dangerous…but for you, I will make this one exception." She turned to look at Daniel, this time with a look of confidence. She outstretched her hands, palms facing him. "Hold my hands and close your eyes," she instructed.

He did so, hesitant at first, not knowing what to expect. A blinding white light pierced his eyes. He wanted to open them but resisted. When the white light had faded, he opened his eyes and realized that he wasn't in his room anymore. The dark candlelit room had disappeared and was replaced with birds chirping and the sun glowing on his face. He couldn't believe his eyes; in front of him stood his house, sunlight beaming through the windows, a bird or two resting on a branch of a tree that was close to it.

The princess smiled as Daniel's eyes widened. She had a warm smile on her face as she said, "We Varinians are born with different abilities. It's not everyone but a good majority of the people you see every day; Balisnor, my mother and father, me. I can go on. I have the ability to not only read your mind, but to talk to you as well."

"Wait, you can read my mind?" His cheeks turned a light pink.

The princess nodded. "I can read your thoughts, your desires." She got closer to him, trying to hold his hand. "I want to make you happy. To clear your head, to give you the motivation you need to continue training."

"Do you…really?" he asked, the emotion to cry constricting him for a minute before forcing it back down. When she had nodded, he smiled and ran to the door, not hesitating to open it. His heart was racing, a smile on his face; he just couldn't wait to hug his mom and dad finally…

There was blood all over the floor, a combination of blood puddles in some areas of the kitchen and blood spatters covering a majority of the walls. *What the hell happened here?* Daniel and the princess slowly made their way through the house alert, cautious, ready to attack at any moment. The cries of a woman came from the kitchen and when he stepped in there, it was as if something had paralyzed him. Like some force had suspended his way of moving about. There was pure and utter terror awakening within him as he walked ever so closely to where the trail of blood was. To his utter dismay and horror, his mother kneeled over his dead father, slash marks on his chest. He dropped to his knees and muttered, "No, no, no."

His mother, head shaking as well as her hands, slowly looked at him with her nostrils flared. "You're the cause of all this," she whispered angrily.

"What do you mean?" Daniel replied with tears beginning to stream his cheeks. "I didn't ask for any of this."

"No, but you are the cause of what is happening. Of what did happen."

"That's not fair…"

"Not fair?" Daniel's mom stood up so fast and began walking toward him. "Don't come to me about what's not fair! It's not fair I sacrificed my living in Varin to protect the so-called prodigal son when his own parents don't want him. It's *not fair* that my husband is dead because of you. It's *not fair* to know that you can't say anything to the royal family without being threatened with your life."

"You know that's not what happened," Anya said coldly, moving next to Daniel.

Daniel's mom ignored what the princess said, getting ever closer to him. In a cold, deadly whisper, she snarled, "Go back to your bastard parents and never come back. You are dead to me."

Daniel was taken so aback, he didn't know what to say. How could she say something so despicable? So heinous? Knowing that he had already lost someone dear and close to him? His knees gave way and he crumbled to the ground; awestruck, in disbelief, all these emotions taking flight. *Is it bad I've already lost Mary, now I have to hear I'm dead to someone that I was trying to protect?* He was so mad, he began crying, wiping the tears out of his eyes furiously. He shook his head, not wanting to be in the same room as this woman.

Daniel stood up and walked out the room, the princess following closely behind. He went outside and breathed in deeply, exhaling slowly. Once Anya had shut the door, he turned to her and said, "Who are my parents, and why did they get rid of me?" Tears were now streaming richly down his face. It was uncontrollable now, no matter how much he tried to fight the urge not to. "I didn't ask for this."

Princess Anya put a hand on her shoulder and said, "The greater the challenge, the greater the warrior. You were born for this Daniel, yet you allow yourself to be incompetent and indecisive over what you want to achieve. The prophecy can still come true…you just have to believe in yourself."

"You didn't answer my question." He grabbed Anya's wrist; the Princess eyed him fiercely and he let go instantly. "I need to know what the hell all of this is. I need to know who I am that my biological parents had to give me to decoys for almost sixteen years of my life, why a vampire chick killed my girlfriend, and this prophecy I know *nothing* about! Make it make sense to me Princess, please! I beg of you!

Princess Anya sighed. "It's hard to explain. I'm not sure if I should explain it to you, to be honest."

"Then who can?"

Anya took his hand and together went back to Varin with Daniel hoping to find the answers to his question.

THIRTEEN

Daniel's mother, or his former mother, sat on the couch trembling uncontrollably, her rage still welling inside her. Her eyes on the floor, rocking back and forth.

"Bravo, bravo," came a voice from the darkness of the living room. "The emotion, intensity…it was lavish to see him crumble."

"Shut up, Penelope," hissed Mrs. Gates as she gritted her teeth.

Penelope tilted her head, her claws slowly growing out. "Now, now. Let's not get complacent. I am the Princess of Darkness. Remember your place."

"I did what you wanted me to do. Now you keep your end of the bargain."

The Princess of Darkness smiled as her eyes turned red, walking to the corpse. Once her long claws had reached his chest, she muttered an incantation that Mrs. Gates couldn't hear. After she had recited it, she stood back to admire her work. The corpse didn't move.

"Why isn't it working?" the woman asked impatiently.

Penelope held up a finger. It was then that the man opened his eyes; but instead of the whites around his pupils, it was all black. The woman stared at the man afraid, not knowing what to do or how to act. "Thank you for contributing to the cause, Tabitha. Your sacrifice will never be forgotten."

"My sacrifice?" the woman breathed, almost in a whisper.

"Of course. I just needed you to break him and you did so extravagantly. Now I have no use for you, and I can always use another Hellhound." Penelope snapped her fingers and watched with glee as the man absentmindedly attacked his wife, ripping apart her stomach and pulling out fistfuls of intestine. In a dark shade of light, Penelope was gone.

FOURTEEN

As soon as he had landed in Varin, he immediately made his way back to the castle.

"You can't just demand to talk with them," the princess said as she tried to hurry to catch up to him.

"Watch me." He ran to the castle, down the hallway and pushed the door to the throne room open. He could see the King and Queen on their thrones talking among themselves.

Out of breath but finally within range to talk he said, "I want to know where I came from, where my parents are, and what's so special about me."

King Erek looked his way, never breaking eye contact as he stood up and made his way to him. "I beg your pardon?"

"I think I made myself very clear, Your Majesty. I want to know more about myself."

Even the smiling King, who he had seen before, was nowhere to be found as he took a step closer to Daniel and said, "That is not how you ask, I'm afraid my child. You would do better to know your place."

Daniel heard the princess approach him from behind, out of breath, and whispered, "What were you thinking?"

The King approached him; Balisnor was behind him but in front of the Queen. King Erek bent down and said in his ear, "Follow me." They walked out of the throne room together and down the hallway, the sun casting an orange hue on the walls as the sun began hiding behind the mountains, the soft clicking of their shoes echoing off the walls, being the only thing that could be heard. When they got to the end of the hallway, the King turned to the right to get in his bedroom. Once inside the bedroom belonging to the King and Queen, Daniel stayed standing near the door, allowing the King to walk past him, going to the dresser to grab two cups and fill them with water. "Sit. Make yourself at home."

The King's room was more spacious than his room, with a square wooden table with two chairs pushed into it. On the middle of the table was a large pitcher of water with tall glasses to the left and right of it.

He sat across from him at the table, folding his hands. "I'm sorry, Your Majesty," he began.

King Erek put up his hand and smiled. For a second, Daniel was taken aback. Daniel took the glass of water the King gave him, trying not to make eye contact.

There was a knock on the door. King Erek sighed before getting up and walking. "Ah, Balisnor. To what do I owe you this welcome?"

Balisnor's voice thundered in the room. "Just making sure you're alright, Your Majesty."

"I believe I'm capable of defending myself in my own room."

"Yes, Your Majesty."

When the door closed again and the King had sat back down, he cleared his throat and took a sip of his water. "So, what do you want to know?"

Daniel took a deep breath and exhaled slowly. "I want to know my lineage. Where my parents came from, where they're at."

The King smirked, pulling out the other chair and sitting down. "And what makes you so unique, am I right?"

"Yes, Your Majesty."

The King cleared his throat and began: "You may not know it now, but you, my friend, are special. You may very well be our last line of defense against one of our most powerful enemies."

Daniel wanted to roll his eyes but refrained from it. He knew he had to be disciplined and stray away from any angry outbursts he wanted to have. This was a perfect opportunity to work on his discipline. He wanted to roll his eyes but refrained. Instead he asked, "Who is he?"

"His name is Mortezan. He has three daughters, two sons, each with different abilities and ways in which they can kill. He used to be one of us, until word got round that he was forming a cult. A cult big enough to overthrow this kingdom. He knows of what you possess and what you will do if he doesn't kill you now."

"What is it that I possess to make me a target?"

The King moved up in his chair, his eyes never leaving Daniel's. "You possess the very thing he fears more, hope. Which is why he sent Penelope after you and when she came back without you; he had her kill your parents."

"But they weren't my real parents. They were a decoy…so who are my real parents? And why did they get rid of me?"

"They didn't want to get rid of you, Daniel."

Daniel scoffed. *She wouldn't have said what she said if she didn't mean it. I'm not sure what to believe anymore.*

The King continued with a gleam in his eye. "They wanted you more than anything, especially your mom. But had they kept you, Mortezan would have definitely had you in his clutches."

"What were they like?" Daniel asked as he poured himself more water, more attentive now that his real parents were being mentioned.

"Your mother had the power to conduct electricity in her hand, your father just had sheer strength. During your mother's pregnancy, there was a prophecy that said that one that had not been born yet would be the one to unseat evil. So, Mortezan being Mortezan, tried to rid you." Erek sighed, putting his head down. "Your parents assigned some friends of theirs to look after you and raise you as their own. Unable to have children of their own, they humbly and graciously accepted. When Mortezan had come and learned of this, he was enraged and burned the whole village down."

A lump formed in the middle of Daniel's throat. *Then, are my parents dead? Or did they escape just in time before Mortezan came?* Daniel cleared his throat, but the lump was still there. "Where is the village? Or where was the village?"

"About a good day's journey. Shinguard is the name of it. You can go there if you'd like."

"I'd very much like that, Your Majesty." He leaned over and said, "I know I just got here and I don't know very much about your culture, but from this moment forward, I'm going to do my best."

The King smiled. "I know your journey has been full of obstacles and pain, but this can be your moment to shine. I will make this oath to you: show me that you can do Balisnor's training and I will make sure that when you complete it, you can go to Shinguard."

Daniel nodded his head, his confidence high and his focus reinitiated. "You got yourself a deal."

They stood up and shook each other's hand before Erek showed Daniel the door. "Good night Daniel. See you at training tomorrow."

FIFTEEN

This is far too easy," Penelope said to herself as she stood at the tree line, watching the wall for any sign of weakness. From what she could see, there were at least half a dozen openings vulnerable for attack. Her eyes turned red and at once she was met with her Hellhounds at her side, snarling, their ears cropped back. "I could take all of them just by myself. Look at them my loves: pathetic, lustful, and so full of fear. They have been enjoying this disgusting peace for a hundred years. I say we feast on their fears and make them relive their nightmare again, yes?"

The Hellhound to her right let out a deep growl in return, revealing its massive and sharp canines.

"Atta boy. But unfortunately, we can't. We have to spy and hide like the shadows. Stay here and don't let nobody know you're here. Mommy will be back soon." With a flick of her wrist above her head, a black cloak enveloped over her, settling on her head to where her eyes were covered and so were her hands. The cloak went to the bottom of her pants, inches from the ground. As she began to walk toward the castle, she looked up and saw the tower shining from the sun. She snarled herself as she continued through the gate, the guards oblivious to who had just entered. *Step one is done*, she thought to herself. *Step two, look for the brat.*

SIXTEEN

When Daniel had made it back to his room, he closed the door and fell on his bed, rejuvenated over finally learning who he was and what he was meant to be. There were no more secrets, no more lies as to what his identity would look like, *could* look like. He, out of all the young men, would be the one to bring down Mortezan. Now he felt like he had to learn more about his enemy and his tactics before anything else. Where he would get that information he didn't know, but he was determined to find out quickly.

"You seem happy," came a familiar voice to the right of him.

Sporting a big grin on his face, he sat up and said, "I think you need to find a better hiding place, My Lady."

Princess Anya came out of her familiar hiding spot and said, "You need to be more careful."

Daniel eyed the Princess suspiciously. "Why do you say that?"

The Princess looked on both sides to make sure nobody was coming. "Can I be honest with you and this stays between us?"

Daniel's heart stopped for a brisk moment, forcing him to catch his breath. After a brief moment, he said, "Whatever is spoken, I won't utter a word, My Lady."

Anya came closer, Daniel got to his feet because he felt he was being rude sitting down. "I feel like I've known you all my life. There's just something about you that pulls me toward you, and I can't explain it. Whatever the reason is, I don't plan on you straying too far away from me."

Daniel's heart skipped a beat over what she had just said. *She what? I mean, she's been close to me since I've been here, but I guess I haven't been paying attention.* He cleared his throat as he replied, "You barely know me though, Your Grace." *Not that I'm complaining, I love it.* He instantly thought of Mary, making him block out any sort of romance towards the princess; which in turn made him clam up again.

In reply, she leaned into his ear and whispered, "I know."

Daniel walked the princess to the door, opening and standing to the side, doing his best to not make eye contact with her. He did not know how to go about with this situation; the last thing he needed was to get in trouble with the King for fraternizing with his daughter. Deep down, he wanted to say something that he was interested too, but for the time being, he could not find the words. The past was still too much of a burden for him to think of anyone else to love at the moment regardless of the fact of how he felt. As the Princess walked slowly past him, he whispered, "Good night My Lady."

SEVENTEEN

Daniel woke up early the next morning, washed his face, got dressed, and began to go downstairs to get to the training grounds before anyone else. Once there he began to stretch, bending down to touch his toes for a few seconds.

"I see someone woke up motivated," Balisnor's voice sounded from the distance.

Daniel shook his head. "Found out the people I've been staying with for sixteen years didn't even want me. That and the fact that they weren't even my parents and that they're some place else, well that lights a fire under your butt. Sooner I do your training and pass, the sooner I can go looking for them."

Balisnor looked troubled, but his voice would not betray him. Balisnor too shook his head and replied, the wooden sword outstretched in his hand for Daniel to take. "Very well. Let's get to training."

During the course of the day, Balisnor taught Daniel how to shoot a bow, teaching him the basic fundamentals of shooting his shot accurately. The first ten shots either missed the target entirely or was off by a few centimeters. After an hour of practicing with the bow and arrow, they went back to perfecting his sword fundamentals from the day before. From sunup to sundown, they trained tirelessly, Daniel taking out most of his anger and depression on Balisnor. Practice ended when the sun was beginning to set, their shadows lengthening.

Daniel and Balisnor were sitting at the stairs of the castle catching their breath. Balisnor got on his feet and patted him on the back. "Better today than you were yesterday Daniel. Keep it up and you'll see yourself in our ranks fairly soon."

Daniel nodded. He couldn't help but smile. "Thanks."

"What was your motivation?"

Daniel shrugged. "I guess not being able to go home, that this is all I have. Might as well make the most of it and give it 110%."

"Keep that going, because tomorrow you're going to fight for real. It won't be against me though. Princess Anya volunteered herself to fight you. Don't underestimate her. So, get some rest and I'll see you tomorrow."

As they separated for the day, they didn't get to see who was peaking from the wall behind them. Penelope had her eyes dead on Daniel, never wavering. When he had disappeared down the corridor, she put her head back down and followed.

EIGHTEEN

Mortezan tried his best to stand up, but he was still not at all strong enough to do so. He growled in resentment as he sat back down staring at his dark dungeon. *This form is irritating me. I need to get back to full strength.*

"Why do you do that to yourself Father?" a voice came from behind him on the side. "Beating yourself up over Penelope's failures. You're the Dark Lord."

"What is the reason of you being here?" Her hands massaged his shoulders as her breath chilled his ear.

"Father, I am your firstborn. I know how to inflict pain, how to make others hurt. I learned from the best. Let me finish what Penelope started. I, unlike her, will not fail you."

"You will get your shot soon enough. Besides, you know that your sister isn't as strong as you."

"Yes, but still." She let go and backpedaled her way to the darkness. "We're in this dungeon because of their incompetence. We do not need to be incompetent ourselves. I will finish the job quickly." Her dark red eyes were the only things that were visible. "I'm here if you need me."

Dark, silent, and alone again, Mortezan grew anxious and rage filled instantly. He let out a deep yell that filled the abysmal dungeon he was in, waiting for the first opportunity that he would be at full strength.

NINETEEN

*T*he sky was a mixture of orange and yellow, the wind whipping his face with heat. Suddenly, a voice erupted from inside the house, but no figure was present along with it.

"How does it feel, knowing your parents didn't even want you? Real or adopted?"

He knew who it was instantly, his senses now at high alert. "Why don't you come on out here and ask that to my face Penelope?"

Penelope laughed, making Daniel even more upset. "Why, when bringing up your past is so much more fun than battling? Tearing up your psyche is what makes it so pleasant. Tearing you down is the thing I crave my young friend."

"So, you're a coward?"

"Oh, far from it. Why would your real parents give you away? So sad."

"Stop. I...I'm sure they had their reasons."

This time, Penelope laughed maniacally, the house ringing with her crazy laughter. "You're so naïve young one. The only one who knows is my father. He knows all about you, Chosen One. Come with me and get all the answers to the questions your heart desires."

"I'd rather die than be one of your cohorts. I've heard what your father's done and want no part of it."

"That can be arranged." All he heard was the wind howl in the silence, then she leapt out with such ferocity that he had no time to

react.

He jumped out of bed, beads of sweat profusely running down his face, short of breath as if he had just run a marathon. He tossed the blankets off him and to the side, making his way to his dresser where there was a pitcher of water and a cup beside it. Pouring it into his cup, he raised it to his lips to take a drink. The water was cool and fresh as it slid down his throat with ease; his mind couldn't help but to think of how amazing it tasted so late in the night like this.

"You're an interesting man my young friend," a voice started from behind him. As soon as he turned around and realized who it was, he was up against the wall with a sharp knife to his throat. "You scream or cause a commotion of any kind, and I will drink your blood while you watch. And believe me, I'm rather famished at the moment."

Daniel was awake, his heart beating faster than a cars piston going back and forth. Looking into her slotted eyes and realizing she wasn't playing with what she said, he nodded. Penelope slowly took her hand off his mouth and backed away, her knife still at the ready.

"I just came to chat," Penelope said as she lowered her dagger, a bit more relaxed. "Having me travel all this way to this godforsaken land is not nice Daniel. You should've just let me capture you back in the human realm."

"Why are you here?" Daniel asked, backing away to the window.

"First off, it wouldn't be in your best interest to do that. I'm evil, not stupid. Second, I wanted to see how the Chosen One is doing in his training."

"And?"

Penelope sighed. "And you, my dear boy, have a lot of training to do if you plan on beating my father."

"The dream. You were talking to me in my dream as well. Why?"

She smiled her evil smile before bothering to answer back. "That's my idea of having fun." She took a step toward him, her knife now in its sheath. "My father knows everything about you Chosen One, from the moment of birth until now. My father knows the answers to the questions you seek, yet these people are restricting you because they're afraid of you acknowledging who you really are. Who you truly can be capable of being with the right training. Sure, they're training you nicely and tending to your every need, but that's because they don't know who you are, how powerful your lineage is."

"Why would I trust you after you killed…them?" Daniel closed his eyes. He couldn't bring himself to say *parents* even though that was who they were to him since the time of birth. They showed their true colors when stuff had hit the fan and now, he had to learn to turn away from them before it crippled him from the inside.

"Daniel." Penelope closed in on him, her smirk clear as ever across her face. "Just because we're on opposite sides of the spectacle doesn't mean we don't share some of the common beliefs. We just…what's the word? Act out more. These people, these Varinians, are scared to see my father rise back to power. They're desperate to find an answer to his chaos once and for all, and all they have to show for it is you. Come with me. Talk to my father. Gain the answers you seek, and see what side is more sinister once you have been shown the Path Before. All you have to do is take my hand and we will go now."

Daniel thought long and hard about it. If it was a trap, then Penelope was laying the groundwork for him to come across it rather perfectly, waiting for the right time to lock the cage and trap him. However, at the same time, if she was telling the truth, then why not go and confront the villain himself? Why not go there and ask him the reason why he was being targeted? It sounded absurd and he knew this wholeheartedly, but he sure wasn't getting the answers from Erek or the Queen. He had to know. He was hesitant to go with her, but he felt like the King was holding something back. *I have to trust her, or at least until I come back. It's not like I don't trust what the King said. I just need a second opinion, that's all.*

TWENTY

Daniel appeared in a dark room that was devoid of the light. He could feel Penelope next to him due to her brushing her arm against his other than that, he couldn't see past his fingertips. There were constant deep growls echoing off the walls, all around him. Penelope guided him along the pathway, stepping on goodness knew what was crushing under his feet. Still, he had no choice but to trust her, even if it wasn't wholeheartedly.

They stopped and Penelope said, "Bow."

Daniel did what he was instructed and went down on one knee. Cold laugher made the hairs on the back of his neck stand up. He kept his eyes on the ground out of instinct, doing his best to keep his breathing under control despite his heart quickening.

There was a voice that echoed all around the room he was in, making it difficult for him to pinpoint the location of the source. "The Chosen One himself. You look…smaller than I thought."

Daniel's heart began racing, his mouth like cotton balls it was so dry. He began questioning his decision to come; he was vulnerable, exposed, and nobody knew he was here to help him. *What have I done?* He gulped his fear in as much as he could and said, "Penelope said you would help me answer questions I have. Here I am taking her up on her offer."

"And what makes you think I would help a filthy Varinian seek out his purpose in this life?" the disembodied voice asked menacingly. "You don't even know who you are fighting for. Do you fight for revenge? Or do you fight for something else entirely Daniel? To understand the prophecy, you have to know how it began. Not follow blindly just because someone tells you to."

Daniel gritted his teeth. "Then tell me!"

A supernatural force threw him off his feet as he slammed into a pillar, breaking off a chunk in the process. Daniel gasped in pain, his vision becoming blurry as something held him in place. "Look how weak and pathetic you are," the voice hissed. "I am the source of your nightmares, of your pain, *of your death.* You symbolize the one thing that was taken from me so many eons ago: love, hope, the will to live. I will not stop until I have what is mine, and not a soul in the Kingdoms will deny me that right." Before Daniel could have a chance to respond, the voice said, "Get him out of my sight Penelope."

Her cold hand latched onto Daniel's elbow and took him out of the dungeon in a flash of light. The sharp pain in his lower back was enough to make him close his eyes as they teleported through space back in his room ten seconds later.

Penelope hit him on the back of the head, making Daniel open his eyes. He was back in his room, the vampire on a knee in front of him. "If you have any more questions about what was brought up, you might want to talk to the big guy. He would know all about what happened. Don't expect this kind of first class treatment again." She got to her feet, looking down at Daniel as she did so. "Next time I'm this close to you, I'm slicing your neck open."

Penelope vanished instantly, just in time to see Princess Anya storm into his room. "Where were you?" she asked, out of breath.

"Getting answers that your parents haven't given me yet," Daniel replied, his nostrils beginning to flare.

"And who exactly did you go to?"

Daniel scoffed at the Princess, turning his back to her. "It doesn't matter. Not like he was much of a help anyways. He wouldn't tell me my purpose in all of this, why they left me or, for that matter, where they were."

Princess Anya stepped toward him. "Who did you go to?"

He couldn't bring himself to say who he went to and knew his downcast gaze betrayed him. When he looked deeply, pleadingly into her eyes, it felt like she was staring into his soul, burning a hole in the center of it as she did so. She gasped and took a couple of steps back. *How could you?* she asked in his mind Before he had a chance to defend his reasoning, she turned to her guard and said, "Arrest him and put him in the dungeon."

The guard did as he was ordered. He apprehended him, led him right out of the castle, down a flight of stairs, and into a torch lit hallway.

With the Princess leading the way, he tried to justify his case. "I still had questions after the talk with your dad," Daniel said, struggling to get out of the grasp of the guards but to no success. "I could sense your dad wasn't telling me everything like he should've! Princess, please!"

The Princess ignored him and continued down the cold underground dungeon.

The smell of mold quickly filled his nostrils as he was led down to a vacant chamber to the left, where the guard unshackled him and threw him into the cell. The metal clang of the door, followed by the click of the key told him that this was real.

He grabbed the bars as he saw the Princess stare at him from the corner. "I need you to listen Princess. This isn't what it seems. You're blowing this thing way out of proportion. What did 'a big guy' do to the one I'm supposed to kill? How does this tie in with me?"

Princess Anya walked slowly toward him, the guards eyeing them carefully with their hands on the hilts of their swords. In a barely audible whisper, she asked, "Why don't you ask your new friend?" She walked briskly away, leaving him speechless.

He went to the cot that was pushed up against the wall and lay there, staring at the aging brick above him through the flickering candlelight. *Who's the big guy he was referring to? How do I represent love, hope, and the will to live? What happened to him that makes me the target behind all of this?* His mind was overfilled, not knowing where to start. He had to get to the bottom of every question and then some to even be able to get a glimpse into how this tied in for him; but in the meantime, he was too bewildered to think about anything else rather than in the now. For the first time, he was alone. For the first time, he was confused. For the first time since arriving in Varin, he was now in jail.

TWENTY ONE

Balisnor was so furious, he was pacing rather aggressively back and forth, his hand on his sword and breathing heavily. He was blind with rage, half of him wanting to cut Daniel down, the other half wanting to beat him to a pulp. Either one of these he knew were both wrong, but he did not care. He turned to the King and said through gritted teeth. "If he were a Varinian, he would be tried for treason and beheaded. What do we do since he's not?'

The Queen snapped her head in his direction. "Beheading him wouldn't be the best outcome," the Queen said, eyeing Balisnor closely. "And under no circumstances are we beheading the only prodigal son who might be able to kill the Dark Lord for good." "Might." Balisnor scoffed, his gaze now fixated on the Queen, his eyes crazy with fury. "There is a fine line between might and will." *He went to the enemy! He needs to be punished!*

Princess Anya walked into the bedroom that instant and said, "He's in the dungeon." She was clearly distraught, her mind elsewhere as she dropped into a chair.

"Let me beat it out of him," Balisnor said instantly. "I will find out the reason why he did—"

"With all due respect Balisnor, I believe I am the only one capable of talking to him."

"Princess, I don't think that's a good idea."

The Princess scoffed. "I know him just a tad bit better than you, in some aspect. And, for the record, what you think is totally different from what I know I can do. I'm not a little girl anymore Balisnor. I was taught by the most excellent teacher. I can take care of him."

She saw Balisnor walk out of the room, cautious to not slam the door.

Balisnor went to the top of the stairs, looking out at the beauty of the world around him, of the stars littering the night sky as the crescent moon shone upon the lake. He had come to be fond of Daniel; from wanting to pulverize him to a bloody mess the first day to cheering for him as he learned the basic techniques of swordsmanship, he was developing a soft spot for Daniel. He was clearly distraught about finding out the news about him going to converse with the enemy. *Does he not trust us? What was the reasoning behind this?* He looked up at the glittering sky and said in a whisper, "I'm doing my best to keep him safe, and I will continue to do so."

He let out an exasperated sigh as he left the stairs and headed toward his room. *It's been one of those days. I need a drink.*

TWENTY TWO

The princess stood in front of his cell, not saying a word as she watched him lay on his marble bed. Watching him shiver and curl into a ball to attempt to stay warm was not what she wanted; she felt awful for doing this to him but…true Varinian or not, he was under the same guidelines as her people. No matter how she felt, she knew that she had made the right decision.

She cleared her throat and said, "I would not have expected this from you. Being able to glance in your eyes and see what you've been doing is my essential power. Why? Why did you do it Daniel?"

Daniel jumped out of his cot and made his way slowly toward her. "If you can read my mind, you know why."

"Desperation gets you killed. I understand why you did it, I really do. But going to the enemy for answers was an idiotic choice. What did he tell you?"

Daniel scoffed, his hands on the bars. "A whole lot of nothing. Couldn't even tell me why my parents didn't want me."

The Princess looked down, not wanting him to see her pity aimed at him. Maybe it was really time for him to know where he came from, what he was. After a minute of breaking eye contact with him, she looked at him again and replied, "You deserve to know." Her hand appeared from her cloak that she had worn to avoid detection and in it was the skeleton key to his cell.

Once he had been unlocked, he stepped out of the cell and made his way out of the dungeon with the Princess, moving with her step for step through the shroud of darkness of night.

When Daniel had made it to his room, Princess Anya said, "Meet me in the throne room in half an hour."

Daniel nodded, then proceeded to shut the door.

Exactly thirty minutes later, Daniel was in the throne room with the King, Queen, and Princess, doing his best to avoid eye contact with Balisnor.

Despite what he had done, King Erek greeted him with a smile. "Sit. We have much to discuss."

Daniel followed the King and sat across from him, the Princess and Queen sitting on either side of him. He did his best to not act nervous as he saw the bodyguard slowly come up and stand behind him. His mindset was telling him that he wouldn't be surprised if he tried to behead him right then and there.

The King was the first to speak. "So, what would you like to know first?"

Daniel reached for his cup of water and took a sip before replying. "Why am I so important? Where did I come from?"

"My, my, you are filled with questions," Queen Guinevere said, laughing as she too reached for her water.

"Your parents were born here," the King started. "Ferocious fighters, loyal to the Crown…wherever they went, they made friends everywhere. Before we knew it, they had made unsuspecting alliances with the elves, dwarves, and the Sucrkai, Dragon People."

"What happened?"

This time, the Queen was the one who spoke. "When your mom got pregnant with you, Mortezan had sent assassins to kill you. Mortezan saw you as a threat simply for the fact that he was almost killed by your mother. Her having you would definitely finish the job she started."

"Who's Mortezan?"

"Mortezan—" the King was about to speak until his wife held up her hand slowly, eyeing him.

"One thing at a time, love. We don't want to overwhelm him"

The King nodded and looked down at the floor. The Queen smiled at Daniel as she continued. "You see, every generation of Varinian is more powerful than the last; which means you would have been stronger than your mom and dad combined. Your mother was terrified and asked if she could hide in the castle walls until the threat passed, but your dad thought better of it."

The King interrupted her. "Mortezan is the one who sent the assassins after your family.

He talked her out of it and told her they would be safer among the Dragons. They ventured out to a nearby village, gave birth to you, and we never saw them again."

The King cleared his throat, looking down as if ashamed at what he was about to say next. "With your parents gone, it wasn't long until the bonds to the elves and other species severed. I, uh, forbade everyone to make contact with them ever again; I realize now how terrible of a decision that was. Forming a bond with the Sucrkai is challenging. We might never get the opportunity to do it again."

The Queen outstretched her hand to hold her husband's, looking into his eyes as she said, "We might have a chance to do right if you fulfill the prophecy."

"What does it say?"

The Queen looked at him and smiled in reply. "The prophecy

states that there is but one who can unite the people and take down the Darkness of the World once and for all. You are the link to make the chains strong again. That's why Mortezan fears you…"

"What is the Darkness of the World, and what does it entail?"

The King shifted uneasily in his seat, looking at his daughter as if she was supplying his words. "The Darkness of the World is a cataclysmic event that will affect all realms, not just within the Five Kingdoms. When Anya was a baby, Mortezan promised that she would fulfill his mission by making her his Dark Queen. If he does that, Mortezan will succeed in conquering everything we know. We cannot allow that to happen."

"He didn't seem like he feared me when I went to go see him." Daniel took another sip before turning his gaze to the King. "You told me that my parents were here in some nearby village. Where exactly is it?"

The King turned his wedding ring on his finger nervously, pacing up and down the room. "I haven't been entirely truthful since your arrival. I said that in order for you to stay. Your parents used to stay at the nearby village of Shinguard but, like my wife said, once your mother got pregnant, they decided to live elsewhere."

Princess Anya shifted her seat to face Daniel, her piercing emerald green eyes gripping his intently. "We're desperate. People here are starting to lose hope. Even though it's been hundreds of years since the Great War, people still hear about the prophecy. We need them to have faith in us, or we're going to lose what we've been fighting for soon."

Daniel had put his drink down. "The Great War?"

"The Great War was between the armies of the Five Kingdoms and Mortezan's colossal army. It was fought about a hundred or so years ago; your parents and I fought side by side right outside this wall. Your mother was so fantastic. She almost killed Mortezan on the spot until he broke away and ran."

"Where is Mortezan from?"

The King closed his eyes and breathed in a shaky breath, waited a moment, then slowly released it. "He used to be a Varinian until my father found out he was plotting against the Crown. He was banished, but he told everyone—man, woman, and child alike that he would one day rise from the Darkness and take the throne. You see, Varin is a part of the Five Kingdoms. It's a stronghold; if we fall, the other Kingdoms fall as well. We can't allow that to happen."

"What was it that made him want to say that?" *There has to be a reason.* "It doesn't make sense. If my mother could almost kill Mortezan and end this thing before it even started, then clearly there's something that I'm still missing. On top of that, he mentioned how *your* daughter would serve as his Dark Queen when the time came. I got all these puzzle pieces intact but I'm missing just one more piece to put it all together. Is he your dad's son? Did your dad do something that he didn't agree with? What's his motive?"

The King instantly replied, "There's no need to overwhelm you. I understand you have a lot more questions, but there's too many to continue going. The next time I'm not busy and up to my eyeballs in what is going on among my people, you can ask me more questions."

Now that he asked all of the questions that were bogging him down, all Daniel could do was nod. He cleared his throat before continuing. "I'm sorry for what I did, to both you and the people of Varin. I won't ever do something as rash like this again." He still had a few more questions, but he realized that their personal time was constricted. He reached out his hand to shake the King's. "Thank you for helping me out. Whenever you get more down time, I would like to talk to you more about it." His guilt was eating him whole. Deep down he knew he should not have gone, but his naivety got the better of him to the point where he didn't care how it affected him or the royal family. *I need to think of something to make it right…in some way.*

King Erek stood up, a big smile on his face. "And I am sorry for my inactions for not telling you everything that you deserved to know. Had I not kept what you wanted to know away from you, none of this would've happened. Are you ready to get back into training?"

Daniel stood up and said confidently. "I'm ready."

Back in his room surrounded by some newfound knowledge, Daniel processed the information. Now that he knew the truth about where he came from, he could focus more on training. However, the very thought of the village of Shinguard being so close to Varin stirred some other ideas in him as well. Should he go there, even though he knew that his parents weren't there? It had happened so long ago; they could be anywhere now. However, if they weren't in Shinguard, he would have to go back to square one and start all over. He had to put it to rest. *I just as well might,* he thought. *No harm in trying.* As he lay down for the night, he couldn't help but to see his parents as ferocious warriors that fought for the same crown he was under. If they did it, then did that mean he had to as well, to live in their legacy? He wanted to think about it but for now, the answer was obvious. He would do it. As his eyes grew heavy and would eventually win the battle of closing, Daniel pictured his parents side by side fighting Mortezan. That in itself put a smile on his face.

TWENTY THREE

I gave you a simple mission, and you can't even accomplish that." Mortezan was livid, his red eyes blazing.

"What do you mean?" Penelope asked, baffled by what her father was saying; she had given him the opportunity to kill Daniel on the spot, yet he didn't. And now she was getting the heat of it. She hissed in dissatisfaction, her eyes like slits. "I practically gave him to you on a silver platter. You failed to act on killing him."

Something from the darkness grabbed her by the throat and pushed her up against the wall; the impact that she had obtained caused her to lose her breathing for a second. It wasn't her father who was choking her. She could feel the arm that was doing it. No, it was somebody else.

"Watch how you talk to father."

"Raven!" Mortezan yelled.

The one known as Raven let go instantly, but not without staring Penelope down as well. Once Penelope had regained her composure and her throat was back to normal, she continued. "The boy is beginning to train," she said as she massaged her throat. "He's a quick learner, much like his father."

Penelope hissed at Raven venomously, getting out of her sister's grasp. "You think you're better than me in everything, don't you?"

Raven laughed uncontrollably. When she had regained herself, she cleared her throat and said, "I don't think I'm better than you, I know. I've been around Father since the Great War. You didn't come in the picture until later." She closed in on Penelope, whispering in her ear, "And you're not even blood."

Penelope's long claws reached around and sliced her in the cheek, making her bleed out a little, but not before regenerating at a rapid pace. "That's not what Mortezan has said. What happened to us wanting the same thing? You were someone I could trust in my times of distress or to get the mission done in whatever was asked of us to do. What changed?"

"You try too hard to please father." Raven smirked, backing away a couple of meters. "I get the job done same day. You like to play with your food before you eat it, to the point where they're begging to die."

Penelope nodded, retracting her claws. "I'll show you. I'll show you how much of a fighter I am, how father can come to me as well and I will get the mission done. Just you wait."

"I'll be here," Raven replied bluntly, heading back into her dark corner.

Penelope shook her head before turning her head to her father and asking, "Any signs of his powers?" Mortezan asked.

Penelope shook her head. "No, but their bodyguard knows how to bring them out. It'll be just a matter of time."

"Keep watch of how he progresses. Let me know of any changes."

"Yes, Father."

TWENTY FOUR

Early the next morning, Daniel woke up before everyone else and made his way to the training grounds. The sun had not yet broken the horizon; an orange tint embellished the sky, showering the mountains in its grace. The cool air that swept through helped to wake him up, brushing his hair gently.

Once on the training grounds, he retrieved his wooden sword and began going back to his previous lessons of parrying and working on his stance, trying to master the different techniques before he could see Balisnor coming from the hallway. Somebody in a cloak was walking alongside him, keeping up with the Bodyguard's pace at which he was walking.

When Balisnor and Daniel were within proximity to each other, Daniel bowed to show his respect. Balisnor, however, ignored him and moved past, bumping him in the arm as he did so.

"No time for morning greetings," the Bodyguard said bluntly, firmly. "Today, you will put your skills to the test." He nodded to the cloaked person.

The being in the cloak took off its head cover, revealing the princess. Daniel tried to keep a steady composure but the fact that Balisnor would even think about matching him up with the princess herself was ludicrous. Princess Anya, however, looked determined and ready to fight.

"Let's see what you've learned," Balisnor said with a smirk on his face. "Don't let the good princess fool you. She can dance with a sword better than most men in my army." Once his eyes met Anya's and he nodded, she ran toward him full force.

What the— Daniel didn't have enough time to react; his blade met hers, causing sparks to fly from their blades. He tried to remember what to do in what type of situation, but with how quick they were fighting, he was having a difficult time. With every swing of her blade, Daniel sidestepped, parried, blocked, or all three. His breathing became steady as he was able to read her movements, his training coming in clutch. She was quick, quicker than him in every regard, but he found himself being able to fend off her attacks. She spun to try to throw him off guard, but he grabbed her wrist and instinctively slapped her, making her lose her grip on her sword. She staggered, holding her nose, sniffling.

"Oh my goodness princess, I'm so sorry," Daniel started as he threw down his sword and ran over to her.

When he had gotten within a couple meters, she reached around and hit him in the nose with her elbow, causing him to lose his balance and fall on his back. Before he could have time to react, the tip of her sword was against the throat. His vision blurry from the tears and warm blood beginning to come out of his nose, Daniel wiped his eyes as he struggled to get to his feet.

"You're fast," Princess Anya said as she lowered her sword, a crooked smile etched on her face.

"Not as fast as you, Your Grace."

"Not yet, but you're very close." The Princess helped Daniel to his feet, brushing the dust off his back.

Balisnor came from behind the princess. "Congratulations, you have passed. Your sword fighting skills could sharpen up just a bit more, but you're a good fighter nonetheless."

"So, does that mean I'm one of you guys?" Daniel asked, hopeful.

Balisnor sneered as he took a couple of steps forward. "Don't push your luck, traitor." He looked Daniel down from head to toe. "You might have them fooled, but not from me. Step out of line again, and I'll make sure my sword runs through your throat."

The Bodyguard walked off, not bothering to look back as Daniel watched him exit out the gate.

"You alright?" Princess Anya asked from behind him.

"Wh—? Oh, yeah. Sure." Daniel scratched the back of his neck, doing his best to not make eye contact.

"Let's go to the lake tonight. Meet me here at sunset."

"Is that even allowed?" Daniel asked, but the princess had already walked off.

If I didn't know any better, I would say she likes me, Daniel thought as he traversed back to his room. The feeling of finally completing his training after so long was immensely satisfying. He was a part of something his parents were once, and to him he felt like he had honored their memory. But what about Balisnor? Would he ever come to terms that he was just trying to get what he needed? Only time would tell but, in this moment, not even Balisnor could take away this moment.

Later that night, Daniel walked out of the castle walls in the shadows of the night, making his way to the lake. What she wanted he had no idea, but he was looking forward to it. The crisp air gently blew in his direction as he ran to the lake, the moon full and illuminating with so much light. It was beautiful to say the least.

He found Princess Anya waiting at the shoreline, the water gently hitting her feet before retracting back in. Though it was a full moon and the light from it made it to where Daniel could see her without any conflict, he only saw that she was wearing a dress that showed off her shoulders. Her hair whipped slowly in the breeze, her beautiful eyes fixated on him and only him.

"Any reason as to why you wanted me to meet you here, My Lady?"

"Do I need one?"

"I-I guess not," Daniel stammered, his cheeks getting hot. Thankfully, though, she could not see it.

"I wanted you to come down here to show you the beauty of Varin, not just inside the gate."

"Won't you get in trouble?'

Anya smiled. "Don't worry about me. I can be quite persuasive. Sit."

They sat next to each other on the shoreline, silent, the scent of her skin—the sweet smell of lavender— filling Daniel's nose. He didn't know what to say, didn't know how to start a conversation, let alone the Princess of a kingdom. He cleared his throat and tried to break the awkward silence between them. "Varin is a lot bigger than what I thought."

The princess laughed. "It might be big, but I think it's small in my opinion. Though it may be because I've lived here my whole life and know basically there is to offer." Silence fell between them until she too cleared her throat and continued. "I asked you down here to tell you something. I just don't know how to say it."

"Just say it, Your Grace."

Princess Anya smiled as she looked down for a second. "I feel a type of chemistry with you that I have never felt with anyone before. Ever since you've walked through that gate, there's just something that attracts me to you. I understand if you don't feel the same way, but I wanted it to be us so I could feel it again without interruption."

Daniel was taken aback, but the thought of Mary instantly reeled him back in. "I'm-I'm honored My Lady to have you feel this way, but I must kindly reject. Don't get me wrong, I feel the same way about you, but right now isn't a good time." Daniel retrieved the necklace from inside his shirt, allowing the Princess to look at the ring. His heart, at once, felt heavy. "Before I knew of this place and of who I was, I was in love with this one woman. Her name was Mary. We had been together since we started high school, but I never once told her how I felt about her. The day she died, a part of me died too. I feel like I can't let go of the one girl who had my heart so easily for another. I feel the same as you do me Princess, I really do, but my heart hasn't yet healed and I have not let her go. I'm sorry Your Highness."
The princess nodded, though she looked disappointed. "I understand. I'm sorry if I went too fast. I just wanted to let you know how I felt about you. When you're ready, I will be too."

Daniel got up and dusted his bottom off. "This place is beautiful and I will do everything in my power to protect it. I hope to build on the chemistry we have between us. Just please remember that since coming here, I haven't been to her grave. I think I owe it to her to say goodbye one final time and maybe in the process get some closure to move on. Have a good night princess." He bowed his head before departing, leaving her to herself.

TWENTY FIVE

I don't trust him Erek," Balisnor snarled, attempting to keep cool. "Him going to the enemy to seek answers…what are the chances of him doing it again?"

"Now that we've answered his questions, not likely at all. He is one of us, as we knew he would be."

"If you trust him, then that's on you. But for me, I'm not going to hold my breath that he stays on our side. His true colors will come out eventually and when they do, don't say I didn't warn you."

King Erek put a hand on his bodyguard's shoulder and squeezed it. "How long have we known each other?"

Balisnor sighed. "Since we were wee little ones."

"And I've always had your back no matter the choices, haven't I?" Before his friend could answer, the King continued. "I'm asking you to have my back now. He's the one we've been looking for. His questions have been answered. Now, he is our responsibility to mold him into what we need him to be."

"I'm with you to the end old friend," Balisnor replied as he slapped his hand on the King's shoulder as well. "Even if at times I think you're making a bad decision."

"Thank you."

The door busted open and in walked an out of breath soldier, his hand on his waist so he could breathe. After a couple of minutes, the soldier regained his composure and said, "Shinguard is requesting help, Your Majesty. Lord Zucharia says there have been spies patrolling around the village. He says that they're led by one of Mortezan's daughters and apparently she is toying with them."

"Send a messenger bird and tell the Premiere my soldiers will begin getting prepared."

The soldier bowed. "As you wish, Your Majesty."

With the door now closed and the footsteps and rattling of mail far off in the distance, Erek turned to Balisnor and said, "Let's see where the prodigal son's loyalty truly lies. Let us find out who's right."

"Do you want me to go with him?"

"No, I'll have Anya and our new soldier go."

Balisnor's eyes were like daggers as he pierced the King's after he had said that. "Your reason to be steadfast in your decisions will one day cost you."

King Erek smiled, not worried about what Balisnor warned. "Ready their horses. They'll leave by morning."

TWENTY SIX

After some time, they had finally made it to the cemetery. Having to hide every now and again, as well as walking in the alleyway took them down a longer and bothersome walk, but they had finally made it. Daniel was paranoid over the fact that he could possibly be getting watched; he wasn't wanting to take the chance.

"I'm here if you need me," the Princess said as she gently patted his arm.

"Don't worry about me, My Lady," Daniel replied, trying to collect his thoughts. He turned in the way of the Princess and was about to say something else when his mouth hung wide open, as if his jaw had been broken. "H-H-How did you do that?" Compared to what she looked like back in Varin, her appearance was quite different in the human realm. She didn't have bangs as the Princess of Varin did; she instead had long brown hair held in a ponytail. She also had lightly tinted silver eyes compared to her dark green orbs. He kind of liked it, but if he had to choose, he would still pick the Princess version.

"What?" she asked. "Don't like my new look?"

Daniel wanted to answer but remembered what he had come here to do. Slowly, he walked down the road, trying to find out where she rested; the Princess was following closely behind.

Finally, after scouring what seemed to be the entire cemetery, he found her gravestone. **MARY STRICKLAND** were in big bold letters. Below that, in smaller calligraphy, were the words BELOVED DAUGHTER.

Daniel made his way slowly toward the tombstone and kneeled, the Princess staying back.

As the leaves on the trees freely danced in the wind and the birds sang their song, Daniel could not find the words that had been haunting him for such a long time. His heart beginning to break once more, like stitches ripping open; fresh heartbreak welled up in his eyes. *What do I say?* he asked himself. *What do I say when I know that this happened because of me, because of who I am?*

Princess Anya's voice spoke softly in his head. *Say what comes from your heart.*

Daniel nodded, wiping his eyes and sniffling. "I'm sorry I wasn't strong enough to protect you." he said quickly, before he didn't have a chance to say them.

Take your time the Princess instructed. *We're not in haste.*

Daniel took a deep shuddering breath before trying again. "I'm sorry I wasn't strong enough to protect you." Those words were the hardest to say, but he did his best to keep going. "I think about you all the time. I'm trying to make you proud, to move on. Some days are worse than others and it's hard to do that. Your smile, your laugh… it feels so much darker and colder without you." He dug in his pocket and pulled out the picture he had had since getting to Varin, serving as his motivation as to why he was going through with his training, setting it on the tombstone. "If today is my last day in being alive, I want you to know that I will always love you. I won't ever love someone as much as I loved you, though I know you would want me to be happy. I wanted to give this to you to celebrate how much you mean to me. Hope you like it. I realize my calling now, and I promise to make you proud."

Daniel made his way back to the Princess, where she welcomed him with open arms. Her warm embrace was enough to stifle the tears and hurt he still felt, but the relief that he had done the impossible felt like a ten thousand pound had been lifted off his shoulders. There was just one more thing he had to do...

"I need to go to one last place," Daniel said, tearing away from the Princess.

"Where to?"

Daniel stood outside Mary's house, his fingers grazing the ring. He sighed heavily; he didn't think he was ready but if he didn't do it now, chances are he would never. *What do I say to them? They still don't know why she died. If they see me, they might ask me questions that I honestly don't know how to answer.* He closed his eyes for a second, breathing slowly.

The princess tapped him on the shoulder, snapping him awake. He made his way down the pathway, his legs like jelly, his mind telling him to go back. He shook his head. *I have to do this. Just, please don't have them come out. At least not yet.* The sun was in its highest place in the sky, an occasional wind gently kissing the trees as it went by. The house was all white, with a big porch that was at the front of the door. He had been inside it a couple of times; he looked up at the window that used to be Mary's room. The tears began to form, yet he wiped them away and continued.

When he had finally gotten to the porch, he looked back to find Anya at the foot of the stairs; she nodded with a warm smile on her face. He nodded in affirmation before retrieving the letter and putting in the crack of the door, knocking, and then running away. He held onto Anya's hand and closed his eyes. He felt light, felt like a new man. While he was content with how he handled things with Mary's parents, there was some controversy that just would not die. *You handled that poorly. The time is going to come when you're going to have to confront them. Because, in the end, you can't keep hiding in the shadows.*

They landed at a nearby park a few moments later and Daniel instantly sat on the ground to gather his thoughts. The princess sat next to him, putting a hand on his shoulder. "Are you alright?"

Daniel was lost in thought. He nodded, not acknowledging her. "Have you ever had your evil side come out?" His eyes still were on the ground, his voice plain. "On our way back, I heard a voice similar to my own, but colder. This is the first time it's ever happened to me. Am I alright?"

The princess was confused, yet she replied with quick succession. "All the time." She laughed and, realizing that he wasn't following suit, cleared her throat and continued. "But I don't allow it to control me, because that is not the person I am. My actions, how I handle tough situations, what have you, is what I should be worried about. You should too." She scooted closer to him, her fingers inches from his. "Just remember, it does not define who you are. It takes a while to go through a loss like that; just know that there are people who are here for you. Now," she got up and extended her hand, "let's go beat some bad guys up."

TWENTY SEVEN

I grow tired of your incompetence, daughter," Mortezan said darkly. "I should've put Raven up to the task. She would have yielded results by now."

Penelope couldn't help but laugh. In her head, she knew what she was doing. Toying with her prey, though slow and unfruitful to her father, was fun and exhilarating for her. "Yes Father, and where would we be? Daniel would be dead and it would be time to look for something new. Have fun." Penelope scoffed. "I have always done what you have asked me to and then some. Why do you treat me as you do? Am I not one of your daughters?"

"You are, but the way you do things irritates me. You need to quit. Raven doesn't play with what I give her; I expect you to do the same."

"Aw, but I like having fun."

"I'm done having fun!" Mortezan snapped. "I want his head on a platter!"

"No fun," muttered Penelope under her breath. "Very well. May I have my dogs now?"

"Get them out of my sight. Phase Two starts now."

Penelope teleported out of there without another word, clearly annoyed.

TWENTY EIGHT

The walk back to the house was relieving to say the least. The anger and guilt Daniel had been carrying around was gone; facing his demons and being able to finally do what had been eluding him for the longest time was so breathtaking. He could now get back to the task at hand: stopping Penelope.

They went down a deserted alleyway in the middle of town, few civilians walking the streets. Suddenly, halfway through the alley, a dark mist appeared out of nowhere. Daniel hurried to the princess' side and put his arm out to protect her; when the mist had cleared, Penelope wore a big smile on her face, her golden eyes penetrating his intently, her long claws ready to slice her prey apart. "I must admit, toying with you was the most fun I've had in a while. But I'm afraid this is where the fun ends." Penelope winked at him. "Déjà vu, much?"

Daniel scowled, bending his knees ready to attack. Princess Anya, however, was quick to hold him back.

Don't. She wants *you to do something. You're still unfamiliar with your powers. She knows this and still wants you to attack. Whatever happens, stay behind me. Let me do the fighting.*

"But—" Daniel started. She hadn't told her, but there was a slight buzz of energy running down his legs. He didn't know what it was, but it was building up gradually to where when he opened his palm, he could see crackles of electricity running through it. *What in the world is this?* Inside, he was freaking out, but in front of Penelope and the princess, he did his best to try to suppress it until he needed to use it.

Princess Anya snapped her direction his way. Her blue eyes enveloped her entire eyeball. It was a bit disturbing to say the least. "I know what I'm doing!"

Penelope laughed. "Aw, the Princess of Varin finally fights. I think violence is a little too much for you to handle, Your Highness."

Anya whipped out her sai. "Try me, vampire!"

She ran towards Penelope, issuing out a war cry as she did so. They met halfway; sai and claw locked in as one. Anya kicked her in the shins, weakening the grasp Penelope had. The succubus stumbled back but before she could regain her composure, Anya dealt a nasty right hook to the side of her face.

Penelope laughed, though a little more maniacally than last time. "You can hit princess. Now let's see how you fair with my babies." Penelope let out a shrill whistle and almost instantly howling and barking echoed all around them.

Daniel and Anya slowly backpedaled but it was too late. Numerous Hellhounds circled around them, too many for them to count. Their large scaly frames glowed a fearsome red in the sun, their large canine teeth sharp and ready to tear prey apart limb by limb. When they had reached a dead end, they turned around and looked at the advancing dogs, who now stopped and walked slowly toward them. Some licked their teeth, others growled menacingly, head and body low, getting ready to pounce.

"Too bad you won't be around to see what my father does to Varin, Anya. He wants me to save you so you could be his Dark Queen. When my father reaches full strength, Daniel will be as good as dead and when he dies, the prophecy will die along with him. How does it feel, knowing these are your last moments and they're spent wasted here in the human realm?"

"If I'm going down, you're coming with me," Anya said, her voice strong, her words ringing true. "You will not make me his Dark Queen. I'll kill myself before he even gets a chance."

Dark Queen? Daniel stood in front of the princess, determined to protect her at all costs. *If I'm the part of the prophecy that is supposed to kill her father, might as well make the most of it.*

Penelope howled with laughter before saying, "Déjà vu much Chosen One? Remember what happened last time you tried protecting your girlfriend?" She laughed even harder. "Didn't end pretty well for you, did it?"

"No, but this time it will," snarled Daniel. "Because I will kill you this time."

Penelope was about to say something in response but pointed a finger at Daniel instead. "You're making me monologue!" She laughed, shaking her head. "You almost got me—"

Varin! the Princess yelled in her head. She grabbed onto Daniel and, in a wisp of smoke, disappeared.

TWENTY NINE

Daniel and Princess Anya made it back to Varin a few seconds later, sprinting from the forest back to the gate as fast as they could.

Balisnor was the first they saw once they had made it back safely. Daniel rolled his eyes; he already knew he was going to be blamed for what happened. He shook his head. *I'm not going to roll over anymore. Let him blame me. See what happens.*

Easy.

He shot a glance at Princess Anya and saw that she was smiling, now back to her regular self.

"How did it go?" Balisnor asked, eyeing Daniel suspiciously.

"It went well," the princess replied. "Ready our soldiers at once. We might be having company real soon."

"Why do you say that?"

"Penelope was there along with her hounds. She wasn't playing either."

Balisnor turned to Daniel and advanced toward him. "What did I tell you would happen if something went wrong?"

Daniel didn't back down as the massive bodyguard proceeded to get closer to him. He smiled, welcoming his advances. "I must have forgotten. You going to remind me?"

"Now you got some gall on you huh?"

"I'm tired of being blamed for something I can't control."

"That is enough," Princess Anya intervened. "Balisnor, back down at once."

Just then, one of the guards burst through onto the training ground. "You should take a look at this."

"Where are my parents?" Anya asked, not taking her eyes away from the bodyguard until he was a considerable distance away.

"They're doing some other things that need tending to, My Lady."

"Very well."

Daniel, Princess Anya, and Balisnor ran to the top of the stairs leading to the wall. There, they could see the forest, the lake and everything between as far as the eye could see. Black smoke wafted from the right side, swaying to the heavens.

"What is that?" Daniel asked. "What's on fire?"

Princess Anya's next words came out trembling, as if knowing the weight of them would devastate the moment she let them loose. "That's Shinguard."

Daniel held his breath, his heart quickened, his hands and whole body beginning to tremble suddenly…his parents were there. Supposedly. He had to go and find them now. This instant. "We have to go," Daniel stated, trying to keep his head clear but failing miserably. "We have to save my parents."

"Could be a trap," Balisnor replied, his eyes set on the black smoke. "We would be walking right into it."

"I don't care! The whole agreement between King Erek and I was that if I finished my training. I could find my folks. I've done your training! Now keep your end of the deal!"

He's right Princess Anya said. *I'm sorry that you have to hear it from me, but it's clearly a trap. If she lures you out, that's that. You still don't know how to use your power correctly despite the training you've done. We would be at a disadvantage.*

No! He couldn't bear this any longer. He closed his eyes and thought about getting there to Shinguard now, gritting his teeth, clenching his fists. A strange fire erupted inside him and when he looked at his hands, he saw that the blue electricity was beginning to form a ball around his hand. *What is this? Am I inheriting my mother's power?* He was afraid of testing it out, scared that he would burn something down. He shook his head in an attempt to clear his mind, to get back to the matter at hand. Tried as he might be, he couldn't get himself to do it. *I'm sorry* he said to himself. *I'm sorry I couldn't do nothing.* "So, we just watch it burn, is that it?"

"We have no choice." Princess Anya turned her attention to Balisnor. "Tighten security around the wall. No one gets past you or your men, understood?"

"Yes, My Lady."

The Princess walked toward Daniel. *Follow me.*

THIRTY

Penelope sat perched in a tree, overlooking the village that she was focused on burning down. Since her father had told her not to come back without the Chosen One's head, she took it upon herself to take her time in achieving her mission. He was right; she had had her fun. Now it was time to end this. No more games. No more playing with her food, as her father liked to say. *He can be such a buzzkill* she thought as she dug the dirt under her fingernails away. She looked at her Hounds, which lay by her side, ready at any moment for her command.

A rush of wind rushed toward her, almost knocking her off the tree. Her eyes turned the violent shade of yellow as she jumped off the tree limb and extracted her claws. She knew who it was without so much as a second thought. "This is my kill Raven," Penelope hissed. "Get lost, before I have my dogs rip you apart."

Raven smiled, her hand on the hilt of her sword. "Do you really want this to end in bloodshed sister? Father sent me here to make sure you did your job. Consider me your shadow until the mission is complete."

"Does he really not have faith in me?"

Raven laughed, her purple eyes never off her sister. "Is that a rhetorical question? If he did, do you honestly think I would be here babysitting you?"

Penelope had heard enough. She lunged at her sister, her body as low to the ground as she could muster, swiping at her when she was within reach. She saw Raven sidestep, then deliver a crushing knee blow to her stomach, making her drop to the ground and lose her breath.

With the sun on her face and the overwhelming pain in her stomach, Penelope lay there defeated. When she opened her eyes, Raven was standing over her with her sword to her throat, her evil smirk unbearable for Penelope.

"Pathetic how you're done after just one blow," Raven said coldly. "If I wasn't here, you would likely find a way to mess this up."

Penelope slowly went to her knees and took deep breaths so she could get the air back in her lungs. "I just-I just want to make him proud. I want him to trust in knowing the fact that whatever he sets me out to do, it will be done without fail. You being here dampens that, and makes me realize that I won't ever be as trusted and relied upon as you and the rest of our siblings."

Raven had some pity for her sister. What she said was true, but her facial expressions remained the same. "Don't look at it like that. I'll tell you what." She offered her hand to her sister, who reluctantly accepted. Once on her feet, she sheathed her sword and backed away a couple of meters. "I will not interfere with your mission so long as it's going smoothly. If it goes smoothly, I will stand back and allow you to do what you desire. Father will be impressed once he hears that I didn't have to get my feet dirty."

"What's the catch?"

Her older sister smirked. "Nothing. I just don't want to go back to that musty smelling dungeon. We both want to impress father, but I see it more from your point of view of how important and crucial this mission is to you and not me." Raven extended her hand to her sister, who was being extremely cautious. "Do we have a deal?"

Penelope slowly reached for it and, once she had her fingers around Raven's palm, pulled her in to where her other hand had her claws on Raven's throat. "You deceive me in any way and I won't care about what father does to me. I will kill you where you stand." She let go and headed back toward her spot in the tree.

Father treats you the way he does because you're an orphan compared to me and my brothers Penelope heard Raven say to her inner thoughts. She stopped in her tracks with her head down, closing her eyes and doing her best to breathe steadily. She shook her head and went on her way, not giving Raven the satisfaction of the doubt that she was living rent free in her mind.

THIRTY ONE

As instructed, Daniel followed Princess Anya to her chambers; she hastily checked the corridor up and down to make sure nobody was coming before closing the door and locking it. "If I hear footsteps, I'll talk to you telepathically."

Daniel quickly nodded.

I noticed your power coming out of your hand. You do indeed possess your mother's ability. Now you need to control it. Use it as a means of fighting for something you love.

"It's hard to picture what you fight for when the only thing you fought for is dead."

The answer to that is in front of you Daniel. You just have to look for it. The time is coming sooner than we both expect it to happen.

"I'll be sure to find it before it's too late."

Anya nodded, smiling. "Now, what's your plan for getting into Shinguard?"

"I thought you said it was a trap."

"I thought that's where your parents are."

"Doesn't matter. We can't just transport ourselves to it. The guards would see our light."

Daniel left Anya's chamber and headed towards his. If what she was saying was true, then he *had* to figure out what drove him. *Time to do a bit of soul searching* he told himself once he had closed and locked his door. *Time to see if I really deserve being the Chosen One.*

THIRTY TWO

Princess Anya was troubled at the fact that the one boy she legitimately had feelings for didn't feel the same about her was annoying. That and the fact her gut feeling was telling her that he was the one destined to be with her only infuriated her further. *If only he felt the same way towards me. I don't want to come off as too strong, but I'm running out of options.*

But he didn't see it like she did.

To her, it felt like he had no interests toward her at all. She knew it wasn't true, considering the fact that he had told her that, while not in condition to date her, he wanted to see where things took them. If they were destined to be together, fate would let it be. *I need to be patient. I don't want to lose him.*

She stared out at the window, the sack laying abandoned on her bed as she glanced at the sky. The winter storms that had been avoiding them for quite some time had finally come: angry, black clouds swarmed across the naked blue sky fast, engulfing the sun and casting a large shadow over all the Kingdom. *Finally,* she thought to herself as she looked down to see her people closing their shops. *The right weather for my mood.*

THIRTY THREE

We don't want them to know we're here yet," Penelope told her sister. "We stay in the shadows until dusk. Once in, we extract Daniel and teleport out of there."

"Where's the fun in that?"

Penelope growled lowly. "Father said if I didn't come back with his head that he would kill me. If that means having a war, I will do just that. I need your help, not your sarcasm."

Raven laughed, her eyes turning a deep purple before turning into a mist, reappearing behind her. "You need not worry. Father won't be having you killed off today little sister."

"Let's get one thing straight: my goal is to make father realize that I can be trusted with a mission. You will not interfere in any way unless I call you. Do we have an agreement?"

Raven smirked, taking a couple of steps forward until she was in Penelope's face. "I told you I have your back. We need to take father's blinders off when it comes to you. So, let's do this before I change my mind."

The clouds in the sky turned black, thunder moving freely as they slowly approached Varin. *It's going to be a long night Varin,* Raven said to herself. *Not even the rain will be able to put out the fires I start.*

THIRTY FOUR

Shinguard is a depot for us in terms of resources," Balisnor said to the King and Queen in their chambers. "We need to protect them, or else what was the treaty for?"

King Erek was looking out his window, focused on the black smoke that was still lingering in the air. "The treaty was for keeping them in line. However, my gut feeling is telling me it's a trap. A diversion for something bigger."

Queen Guinevere was sitting on her bed, legs crossed, not saying a word the entire time until now. "Balisnor, how long has it been since we've been at war?"

"Hundreds of years, Your Majesty."

"Exactly. The Five Kingdoms has not had to strap on armor and defend what we love for hundreds of years. Why, the last war between us and the Assassins, I was just a little girl." She got to her feet gracefully, making her way to her husband. "Perhaps our people need a reason to defend what they love again. They've been spoiled for too long. I believe it's time to tell them what they should fight for."

King Erek turned to his wife. "How could you condone war?"

"If fighting for what I love is condoning war, then so be it. If giving our people hope instead of running in fear is condoning war, then so be it. Once they start attacking, and they will soon, they will be after Daniel. Why do you think?"

"He doesn't know how to use his power yet," Balisnor replied quickly.

The Queen smiled, never taking her eyes off him. "Right now, they have all their pieces ready to move. What will you do, my love? Will we strategize better, or play freely and see where the dice may land?"

King Erek looked at his wife. She was right. If the Five Kingdoms caught wind that they didn't protect one of their villages, it would prove to be disastrous for them. The rest of the Kingdoms would think they had lost their touch, unable to defend what was theirs and attack. He wasn't about to let that happen. He cleared his throat, turned to Balisnor and instructed, "Ready our troops for battle. I believe it's time to start fighting for what's ours again."

"Yes, Your Majesty."

Balisnor left, leaving the King and Queen alone once more.

THIRTY FIVE

Princess Anya and Daniel met at the common ground right outside the castle a little after the sun had set for the day. The air was frosty, the wind blowing consistently against them was nothing short of unpleasant, but they had already made up their minds. There was no going back.

"Are you ready?" she asked, her fingers curled into a fist.

Daniel nodded impatiently. "Ready as I'll ever be." He grabbed her hand and together teleported out of the safety of the wall, ready to confront whatever was out there.

When they had landed, they realized quickly that the only thing that was on fire was a nearby campfire. They had landed right where they instantly knew was a bad idea.

"Crap," Princess Anya whispered under her breath.

Daniel pretended to be shocked, saying, "Language, My Lady."

Anya scoffed before pushing Daniel playfully, but low growls quickly sobered them. From the trees glowed bright golden eyes to the right, as well as two purple orbs to the left. All around them, though, were smaller orbs of red outlining the trees.

Hellhounds, Anya said in his head. *Whatever you do, don't split up. You won't stand a chance.*

"That telekinesis ability sure does come in handy Princess," he heard Penelope say from somewhere in the shadows. "One I envy even among my own."

Princess Anya's eyes turned a deep shade of blue, her fingers ready to retrieve her sai. "What do you want?" she asked.

It was apparent that they knew what she was trying to do, which is why both the sisters laughed at the same time. "Trying to buy you both some time is absolutely adorable. "

Someone from Daniel's peripheral vision came from the darkness, but he had no time to react. He was pushed against a tree. A black haired purple eyed woman solidified in front of him, smiling widely. "You must be Daniel." She turned to her sister, who had her claws elongated, her eyes on the Princess. "Do we really have to kill him? He's cute."

"I'm afraid we do."

The purple eyed woman turned slowly back to Daniel with her smile still intact and replied, "Shame."

He glanced from behind his captor's shoulder and saw that Penelope was inching even closer to the Princess, saying words that he couldn't hear. *I have to do something.*

Penelope's eyes grew even more bright gold, her tongue hanging out.

Something. He started struggling. *Anything.*

The succubus took the first swing, Princess Anya able to avoid the blow. Penelope rushed her, knocking the princess to the ground.

Come on, you stupid power. He grit his teeth, fighting to get out of the woman's clenches. *Activate! Do something!*

"There's no point," the woman said as he saw her teeth grow out. "I'm going to have you watch the Princess die, then I'll drink your blood, and then attack your pathetic kingdom. I wanted you to watch it burn along with all their hope and joy."

He closed his eyes, not wanting to watch what might fall on the Princess. *Stupid! I'm so freaking stupid! They said it was a trap and I didn't listen.* He opened his eyes a little and saw Anya doing her best to fight off Penelope by kicking and punching wherever was open. She eventually would get overpowered, her hands pinned to the ground with the succubus' mouth open wide.

Anya's words of advice came to life from his head. *You have to think of something that makes you feel like fighting for to summon your weapon.*

As he looked on helplessly, he began to think about something worth fighting for. Of course! It was right in front of him, just like she had said! He closed his eyes again, feeling the woman's fingers begin to tighten around his throat. As loud as he could in his mind, he proclaimed, *Princess Anya is worth fighting for! Varin is worth fighting for!* For the final time, he opened his eyes and shouted, "Being free from monsters like you is worth fighting for!"

A blinding white light overtook all the village. The woman lost her grip His body tingled with heat, numbing him to the core as a result.

When the light faded after a couple of minutes, he saw the petrified faces of Penelope and her sister rather clearly. Princess Anya was on the ground on her hands and knees, her mouth hanging open in awe.

You've done it, he heard her say, her voice trembling with excitement. *You should see for yourself.*

Penelope's eyes grew red with rage as she shouted, "Get him!"

All the Hellhounds, from all angles, began to pursue him. Their mouths agape, their canines ready to rip and tear.

Daniel's instincts had heightened by tenfold. He could smell the pungent odor of the Hounds, hear the talking of Penelope's forces that were a considerable distance away. His sight was impeccably better, able to see every grain of detail in everything he put his eyes on. Every line along the hilt of his sword, the clarity of the sky, it was tremendously vivid. , ready for whichever hound decided to pounce first. One poor hound misjudged his time and lunged for Daniel; he caught it with his bare hands and wrestled it to the ground, its mouth still open. Writhing and twisting the hound attempted to break free, but to no avail as Daniel snapped its jaws with ease, killing it instantly; Daniel got up, dusted himself off and ran toward the Princess. "Let's go!"

He stopped long enough for the Princess to jump on his back before he ran with everything he had back to the gate, the rest of the Hounds scared to pursue him any longer.

Varin! Daniel shouted in his head.

Daniel's feet left the ground, the cold wind no longer stinging his face. *I cannot believe we got out of there alive. That was way too close.*

They touched down a second later, guards and soldiers strapped with their armor ready for battle. None of that mattered. He put Anya down as calmly as he could, making sure there were no scratches on her face or bruises. Not finding any, he put her forehead to his and whispered, "I'm sorry. I should've listened to you."

Princess Anya put her hand on his wrist gently, not wanting him to let go. She closed her eyes and was hoping this moment wouldn't end. "Don't worry about it. I would have done the same thing as you if I were in your shoes. What did you think about when you activated your power?"

Daniel could only smile as he parted ways with her, helping her to her feet. All he could say was, "You."

Before they could say another word, Balisnor, King Erek, and Queen Guinevere walked up to them, their expressions grim, Balisnor's expression especially deathly.

Queen Guinevere looked at the both of them and said, "I assume that white light was you?"

Princess Anya looked down in shame. "That was us mother. I told him we would sneak out and go to the village to go look for his parents, but it was a trap. No buildings were on fire. We fell for it and almost didn't make it out alive."

King Erek was next: "How *did* you make it out alive?"

The princess motioned her hand to Daniel, who was kneeled. "He was able to use his power to get us out."

The three of them were silent, staring at Daniel like they didn't expect it to be true. Then, unexpectedly, they all cheered and patted Daniel on the shoulder.

"Excellent job!" praised King Erek.

"Splendid!" exclaimed the Queen.

"I knew you had it in you," Balisnor said dryly.

Daniel bowed. "Thank you."

"Mother. Father." Princess Anya took a step forward. "Mortezan's daughters are here. We have to prepare for battle."

"Already ahead of you," the King said, smiling. He motioned for Daniel to follow. "I've been saving something for you for this day. Come with me."

Daniel looked behind him at the princess, watching as she went with her mother up the stairs. He wanted to tell her how he felt, but he was afraid that if he did, memories of Mary would pop up and he would be back to where he was at before.

The King turned back and asked, "Are you coming?"

Daniel snapped back and replied, "Yes sir. My apologies."

Together, they made their way to the dark dungeon, the King creating a light with his hand as the darkness swallowed them up.

THIRTY SIX

The sun had peaked over the mountains a couple of hours later, yet Penelope and Raven had been sitting on the ground reminiscing over what had happened hours before.

It was Penelope who had broken the silence a while later. "Unfortunate turn of events if you ask me. We had him, and still he got away. How?" She stood up, rummaging her hair. "How? I should've killed him when I had the chance."

"Should've, would've, could've," Raven replied bluntly. "We both failed in getting what he wanted done. It doesn't matter now. We must get him. I'm going to talk to Father, see if I can get the army ready."

Penelope nodded, leaning back against one of the trees looking at the clear blue sky that had come for all to see. *Another day. Another lost opportunity.*

THIRTY SEVEN

Raven appeared before her father, bowing as she came near. "His powers are out My Lord. We have to attack."

"I've been thinking a lot as of lately…what if I put myself into a Hellhound? So I could do it myself what proves to be too difficult for two powerful women."

"Why on earth would you do that?" she retaliated. "That's an imbecile move. The Hound's body would not hold you for very long."

"Which is why I would have to move fast." Mortezan's red eyes glowed in the dark. "Because apparently my two daughters can't kill one measly, miserable person!"

"Sacrificing your body by putting it in a more vulnerable state is ludicrous!" Raven shouted back. "What if the Hound's body suddenly spazzes out and cripples? All they have to do is put their blade through your chest!"

"I'll take my chances."

Raven rolled her eyes. She wasn't going to continue arguing with her father. *Let him do what he wants then.* "You're right father. That's not a bad idea My Lord. Plus, with you on the battlefield, it would give our troops hope."

Mortezan scoffed. "Hope. What a disgusting word. My presence will be unbearable for the Varinians to take on full force."

"Shall I get them ready father?"

"Yes, but first, fetch me a Hellhound and leave me."

Raven stood up and curtsied. "Yes Father."

THIRTY EIGHT

Daniel followed King Erek past the cells and deeper underground. It was so dark Erek's hand sparked a fire, making it a lot more bearable to see where they were going.

"Your father and I always snuck down here to cause trouble." Erek laughed to himself. "One time, we got stuck down here and ate only ants and baby scorpions to keep us from starving. Fun times."

"What do you hope to accomplish with the two of us down here together Your Majesty?" Daniel asked, wondering why Erek was being so nice to him.

Erek stopped in his tracks, turning around and smiling...or so Daniel thought. The flickering flame of his hand made it hard for him to see clearly. "I've seen the way you look at my daughter Daniel Gates. And I've seen how she looks at you. It's no coincidence your power came to be back at Shinguard. You have to think of something worth fighting for and that something ended up being her. She has never had that type of chemistry with anyone else, so to see her risk her neck out for you is remarkable."

Daniel blushed and put his head down. "She would've done the same for me."

"Maybe, maybe not. However, I can't turn a blind eye on the fact that the chemistry between you two is what brings out the best in you." He put his hand on Daniel's shoulder. "When we get back to the castle, if you're willing, I give you permission to be with my daughter and fight for her hand next year."

"It would be an honor, Your Majesty. Thank you."

"No, thank you for saving my daughter's life. I am in your debt." Twenty minutes later and unable to see his hand in front of his face, they had made it to a large room. Barren but having what looked to be a chest, he walked toward it, Erek allowing the fire to spread around the wall.

When he had reached the chest and opened it, he noticed something shiny. He grabbed it, pulled out a piece and realized that it was chest armor. It was a deep red color with a gold eagle encrusted in the middle.

"Your dad's armor," the King spoke behind him. "He was so ecstatic over your mother's pregnancy that he did everything he could to save what he once treasured to you.

"I hope it fits. I can't wait to try it on."

The King smiled. "Come, let's go back. We can't leave the women alone for too long."

THIRTY NINE

Princess Anya and Queen Guinevere were sitting side by side in the Queen's chambers, the Queen making sure there were no marks or bruises on her daughter's body.

"Mother, I've already told you, I'm fine," the Princess scoffed, trying to wiggle free of her mom's clutches.

Queen Guinevere sighed. "It really is remarkable Daniel was able to do what he did. Otherwise, goodness knows what could have happened."

"Yeah." She shivered, reflecting back to how Daniel snapped the Hound's jaws like a toothpick. "About that…"

The Queen leaned in closer. "What was it like?"

Princess Anya took a second to answer, then: "For lack of a better word, it was awesome. The last thing I remember is him looking at me. There was a blinding white light, then…his eyes. His eyes were an iridescent red, blue electricity going up and down his arms. And his strength." Her voice was trembling now, though from fear or excitement she didn't know at the moment. "He ripped a Hellhound's jaw out with just his arms."

"That is incredible. Though it's obvious he got his power from you."

"How do you think?"

"Think: he saw you in danger, didn't want to see you hurt, and saved you from dying. He cares for you Anya, whether he wants to admit it or not."

The Princess looked down. "I do as well. I went to his girlfriend's grave to see if that would help, but I don't think it did. I know I shouldn't and that it might be a lost cause, but he's the only one who gets me."

"You have to keep doing what you can to make him see then, don't you?"

"I worry that if I push too hard, I'll lose him."

"When your father and I were younger, he never gave up on trying to impress me." Guinevere laughed. "Even though I tried so hard to ignore his advances, I couldn't."

"Thank you, mother. I needed that."

Guinevere smiled. "Go get what's yours."

FORTY

Mortezan stared at the Hellhound wondering, debating, if this would really work. How he longed to be able to walk again! Though it wouldn't be his own unique body, he would finally have the chance to walk again. *It's time. I need to do this.* He outstretched his hand, saying out loud an incantation from an ancient tongue that had not been used for hundreds of years.

After saying the incantation, he felt the same. No change. Then, piece by piece, he started to flow away into the Hellhound; the hound itself was laying down whimpering.

A few minutes later, Mortezan opened his eyes and could feel the changes almost instantly. It took a couple of seconds to get to his feet, stumbling down the stairs to his nearby table that was centered in the middle of the room. In the middle of the table was a cantaloupe; he grabbed it and with such ease, smashed it between his hands with no trouble. *It worked.* He looked down at his armored hands, sharp talons at the end of them. *It actually worked.*

He admired himself, looking down at his legs and thanking the Elders that he was without the tail. He raised his hand, a thick red mist came to life; a wicked scythe forming in one hand, a sword in the other.

Let's see what this body can do.

For the first time in a hundred years, Mortezan was finally able to teleport out of his dungeon he himself considered a prison. He wanted carnage, and now there was nothing that would stop him from getting it.

FORTY ONE

Daniel was in his chambers admiring his father's armor when he heard a knock.

Gently putting the armor on his bed, he jogged over to the door. Princess Anya was waiting for him on the other side of the door, her smile wide. *What is she so happy about?* he asked himself. "My Lady."

"May I come in?"

Daniel smiled. "I don't know why you keep asking." He let her through, closing the door behind her. "What can I assist you with today, Your Highness?"

"What did I tell you about all that? Please, call me Anya." She chuckled, scratching the back of her head. "I should reiterate that more often. I thought you would have caught on by now."

"My apologies M…Anya."

Anya sat on his bed, patting the side of her so he too could sit next to her.

Daniel did so. Every time her emerald green eyes touched his, it would set him into a whirlwind of emotion. The way all her dresses seemed to hug every orifice of her curves was breathtaking; he felt like every time she entered a room, he found himself having to pick his jaw off the floor. It felt common. It felt natural.

Anya broke the silence. "There's something I want to tell you. I need you only to listen."

"Of course." He still had the urge to say, "My Lady," but he bit his tongue and looked down so she couldn't see his pain.

The Princess took a deep breath, exhaling slowly a moment later. "I know we've discussed this briefly before, but I like you. A lot, as a matter of fact. I know the pain you carry from your girlfriend dying is worse than I can imagine and I understand. However, I need you to understand that I've never felt such chemistry with anyone like I have with you. I feel…" She didn't know her hands were gripping each other until now. Why was she so nervous? She cleared her throat, shaking her head in the process. "I feel like we're meant to be."

Daniel sat there, smiling. Since he was able to go to Mary's resting place, he had been feeling a lot better. He felt like she would've wanted him to be happy, even if it wasn't with her. He grabbed for her hands tightly in his, looking in her eyes. "I'm sorry if you feel I am not interested in you. I think I've told you before that for right now, I want to see where this goes. You know, just until I'm no longer grieving over Mary's death. Thing is, what you've been experiencing has been what I have as well." He took a deep breath, fighting the urge to grab her hands. "Every time I look at you, I lose my breath. I'm always having to pick my jaw off the floor. It's embarrassing, but it's the truth. The thing I have a hard time with is I'm afraid of getting close to you out of fear of seeing her. Every time I try to suppress my thoughts of her and move on and be with you, she comes back with a vengeance. I can't shake her, no matter how much I try. That, and I've just…I've had a hard time putting myself out there since her death."

"It's still fresh too. Only a few months."

"That too. I want you to know that I do care for you, and that I do want to see where this takes us. I just hope you will be patient and wait for me when I'm ready to love again."

"Of course I will wait. All I ask is that you tell me when you are indeed ready."

Daniel smiled, something that had become a common occurrence for him since Anya and him have talked. "That's all I wanted to say on the matter. In the meantime, my job is to keep you safe and out of harm's way; I will do that to the best of my ability."

Daniel watched as the princess got up and held onto his hand. "I really do care for you Daniel. I have since you first stepped foot. You cannot change destiny, or fate, whichever it is that you believe. I will wait for you for as long as I can; all I ask is that you don't keep me waiting."

She left the room, closing the door behind her, leaving Daniel to his lonesome. *I won't keep you waiting Anya. I'll be ready before you know it.*

FORTY TWO

Raven and her father's army hid in the Varinian trees, keeping out of sight. Once she had given orders to the general, she made her way to her sister. "We're ready to attack if need be. Father gave me the army no problem."

Penelope scowled. "You know, just because we agreed on not killing each other doesn't mean my hatred towards you isn't still there. You agreed to be a shadow, so be a good shadow and zip it."

Raven was going to say something in reply to that when a thick red mist appeared out of nowhere, silencing them as it formed in front of them. Raven nodded to a couple of her soldiers and they followed her to the front of the line, waiting to see what was going to come out. Her hand on the ready, she eyed it intently, her purple eyes glowing with anticipation.

Mortezan came out of the mist, his eyes glaring at everyone as he stepped through. He stared up at the sky and closed his eyes, inhaling through his nose and out his mouth. "Varin," he said coldly. "The place where it all started."

"Father," the two girls said in unison.

"Penelope. Raven."

Raven looked at her father, smirking. "You did it."

"It took some time, but yes I did."

"How does it feel?"

"It's not my body, but as of right now, it will suffice." He turned his gaze toward Penelope. "This is still your mission. Ready our soldiers. We're going to battle."

Penelope stepped forward, taking charge. "Yes Father."

Raven was furious. The very thing she had told him not to do, and he went around and did it anyways. *How am I supposed to protect him when he doesn't heed the words that I tell him?* She looked at the villagers and growled, her purple eyes glowing menacingly. She started to shake, her hand on her hilt as she walked toward the front of her army. The way she saw it, if he didn't care about what she told him, she didn't care about what he said to her. She lunged her sword in the air, causing her people to shout and issue out their war cries. She was bloodthirsty; she wanted to unleash her fury. She looked behind her, searching for her father and when she did, smirked in his direction. The line of villagers were ready to defend Shinguard. She smiled, recognizing the overwhelming sense of fear stimulating from them. "But first…" Her eyes glowed red as she charged maliciously toward the village…

FORTY THREE

They haven't budged," Balisnor announced to the King, Queen, Daniel, and the Princess. "That campfire has to be dead now."

"They were literally camped right outside the village," Daniel said. "It was a clever trap."

"Complimenting the enemy now too, eh?" Balisnor asked. He slapped his hands down on the slab of rock and turned to face Daniel. "Why don't you join them then?"

"I don't want you guys to get wiped out."

"Big tough guy now that you have your power, aren't ya?" He grabbed his hammer from behind his back and walked toward him. "Why don't you fight me then?"

"What's your problem with me?"

"You know exactly what my problem with you is. Traitor."

"It was one time!"

"That is quite enough." Queen Guinevere stepped between them, Balisnor's eyes still on fire. The Queen turned to him and said, "Hit him in any way, even unintentional, and I will strip you of your title as bodyguard. He has learned from his mistakes. Let it go."

Balisnor stared at the Queen intently, before bowing and walking off.

"Definitely not the guy to commit a wrong against," King Erek said, laughing nervously. "That man can hold a grudge until the end of time. I would definitely try to make things right, especially if you want to do what we were discussing earlier."

Daniel searched for Anya and when he did, he walked toward her slowly, taking his time with each step. The dream he had had felt so real, Mary felt real. He found the princess staring out past the stairwell, her hands crossed on the handrail. She looked lost in thought, her armor already on, ready to go. Her hair was in a ponytail, with both her sai on opposite sides of her hip. It felt like all eyes were on him in the rear, though he dared himself not to look back. He went on the side of her, looked at her, and said, "I know we haven't known each other for very long, but considering that you're stuck with me, now would be a great time to start. If you would still have me fight for your hand in marriage, I humbly accept your challenge."

Princess Anya looked down, her face blank, making it hard for him to determine what she was feeling. Finally, when she looked back up, she said, "Whatever you feel, I feel too. That doesn't just happen Daniel. The way I've felt about you since you have arrived is more than what I have felt towards anyone else." She turned to face him, her eyes locked on to his, her hair blowing in the wind. She put her fingers on his forearms, closer than usual. Daniel could see out of the corner of his eye that the King and Queen were sure about this, though Balisnor looked as though he were going to have an aneurysm at any moment. "I forgive you." In an even louder voice she said, "Daniel Gates, I hereby choose you, in the presence of my parents and all of Varin, to fight for my hand in marriage. Father, do you bless this decision I have made?"

King Erek stood tall, chest out and declared: "I, King Erek of Varin, accept and bless your decision daughter."

"Mother?"

Queen Guinevere did the same thing as her husband, except she bowed her head in return. "I, Queen Guinevere, also accept and bless your decision my daughter."

Princess Anya turned to Daniel and said in his head, *Do you accept this blessing I have bestowed onto you my future King?*

Daniel went on his knee before the Princess and said, "In the presence of your parents and all of Varin, I accept your blessing and decision for me to fight for your hand."

Very well, Princess Anya replied. *You have come so far Daniel. I'm so proud of you.*

Before any more words could be said, one of the soldiers from his post yelled out, "Movement from the trees! Black smoke everywhere!"

All four of them rushed upstairs and could see smoke billowing far bigger than what it was before. Hellhounds raced out from among the trees and into the open land. After the Hellhounds came, the soldiers themselves marched out to form their vast formations.

Finally, after all the soldiers had made their way into their ranks, three individuals strolled out. Daniel knew two of them at once, but who was the one in the middle? It was buffier than the two girls and looked oddly reddish. To the right of the massive being was of course Penelope, her eyes red. To the left, Anya mentioned that her name was Raven. Her claws were also out, her purple eyes taking full control of her eye sockets.

"Who is that?" Queen Guinevere asked. "The one in the middle. It doesn't look to be any of his three sons."

Daniel looked down where Guinevere's finger was pointing and froze in terror. It was as if all at once his nightmares had come rushing through him. Yet, a strange feeling came over him: along with the terror that sheered through him like a hot knife through butter, there was also the feeling of raw, unfiltered anger that drove him to the point of madness. He didn't look at this man like everybody else had a fearful look on his face; no, this time, it was a feeling like no other.

"Who is that?" Princess Anya, echoing off what her mother asked.

The King turned to face Daniel. "I told you this opportunity would present itself sooner than we both liked or expected it to. The prophecy lives within you."

Wait... Daniel thought as the King made sure his armor was good to go. *Is that...is that Mortezan?*

Princess Anya gasped. She looked at the man more carefully. The spikes on his arms, the reddish glow...something was off about his appearance.

Balisnor growled. "He fused himself with a Hellhound. They're powerful creatures; deadly and lethal and merciless. But fusing one's body with a Hellhound is the most unholy. An abomination."

From the ground, Mortezan walked toward the wall, his hands in the air. When he spoke, his voice boomed. "Daniel Gates! The Chosen One, or so they say! Come down here to fight me or I will make sure I eat the Princess in front of you!"

Mortezan's army was massive; even if the Varinian army could fight them off, they would be overwhelmed eventually. Mortezan was giving them a chance. He only wanted Daniel. If Daniel fought him, then Varin would be safe. If Daniel cowardly walked out of Mortezan's challenge, then all of Varin would burn.

Mortezan's voice boomed again. "Do you really believe you stand a chance against my army? The remaining four Kingdoms are not with you. You don't have a chance. Fight me. You know you want to!" Daniel walked toward Balisnor, not caring if the bodyguard was still upset at him or not. "Whatever I have done to you to have you mad at me, I ask for your forgiveness. If I'm to die today, I want you to remember me by owning up to my mistakes and transgressions I may have caused you. Thank you for training me. I will make you proud."

Balisnor grabbed Daniel by the shoulders and shook him, his eyes still like daggers, his face still contorted with rage. "You're just like your father. He was always asking questions, always got into trouble, but always did the right thing." His eyes began to tear up, making his grip a little tighter. "If it wasn't for the fact that he married my sister…" He wiped his eyes fiercely, sniffling. "Make her proud, as I am. You have her ability to never give up. Defeat him. Keep fighting."

Balisnor pulled Daniel in for a hug before escorting him to the gate, their hands around the other's neck.

When they had reached the gate entrance, they ripped apart, Balisnor holding out his hand. Daniel shook it without a second thought. For the first time, Daniel got to see Balisnor smile. "Kick his ass for your parent's sake, eh nephew?"

Daniel laughed. *This can't be real,* he thought to himself. *The bodyguard of Varin is my uncle!* "Will do."

Balisnor nodded his head, and a second later the doors finally opened. Daniel lowered his head and closed his eyes. "I'm not one for religion, let alone praying. All I'm asking is for you to protect me if it's not too much trouble. Whether it's you, my parents, a random somebody, I don't care. Just get me through this and we can talk about what happens next in terms of us."

When he opened his eyes, the gate was open. He glanced up at the Princess and nodded. *I will come back to you. I promise Anya.*

He could see her smile, which fired him up. *You better. Who else will be my King and by my side?* As he made his way slowly toward the battlefield, he heard Anya say *I love you.*

Daniel looked back and saw her leaning against the wall in anticipation. *I you too.*

Watch out!

It was too late. Mortezan bumped into him, knocking him several meters back. His side hurting, Daniel struggled to his feet, his sword serving as a cane.

"You want to play dirty?" he asked, throwing his sword down and activating his power, his teeth gritted. "Let's play dirty!"

FORTY FOUR

Daniel let out a yell as he transformed into his enhanced self. His size grew by three additional feet, his arms adorned with a type of armor with his fingers being long claws. He felt the familiar current running through him, like a type of battery. He was overcharged, ready to destroy Mortezan's army single handedly. Once Mortezan had closed the gap, Daniel punched him in the stomach, knocking the Dark Lord back. Daniel, however, wouldn't stop. *I need to keep pressuring him. If I let off once, I'm done.*

As every one of his punches found their target, he noticed that Mortezan was laughing. "Is that all you've got Chosen One?"

Mortezan swung behind him, wrapped his arms around his waist and leaned back, smashing him into the ground. With his head buzzing, Daniel lay defenseless with the Dark Lord beginning to claw at the back of his head. There was ringing in his ears, blood dripping from the sides of his head.

The Dark Lord had finally stopped, leaving Daniel somewhat conscious, but the need to close his eyes was weighing on him more and more by the second. He knew that if he closed his eyes, that would be the end.

"Your prodigal son is no more Varin," Mortezan said. "Now all of this wretched Kingdom will burn!"

Daniel.

Anya's voice came awake in his head, the ringing somewhat dissipating. *Daniel. You* have to *get up.*

He wasn't strong yet. He did his best, sure; but his best ended him lying on the ground clinging to life.

You have to get up!

He could hear the urgency in her voice now, sterner than before, desperation as well.

Get up!

"I can't," he said to himself. *The hell you talking about you can't? Your parents didn't die for you to give up on yourself! Get up!*

Get up Daniel!

Get up!

His arms that were on his side began to inch forward; intense pain shot from both his shoulders all the way to his fingers, yet he still fought to get them above his head.

When he finally had gotten his hands above his head, he dug his fingers in the dirt and put all his might, all his remaining strength into standing up once more. "Hey sleazebag, is that all you have?"

Before Mortezan could turn all the way around, Daniel got up and swung frantically at Mortezan, hoping a good deal of swings would stagger him. Momentum quickly shifted from Mortezan to Daniel, with Daniel taking advantage of every opportunity given. He made him hurt. He could see him getting irritated, growling in protest, but Daniel didn't care. Every time Mortezan attempted to counter, Daniel would grab the back of his head and pound it against the ground several times.

Mortezan began to slip into unconsciousness. Daniel lifted his hand one last time to give the final blow when something tackled him down.

Penelope had rolled off Daniel and stood up, hissing. "It was fun while it lasted. Now it's your turn to die."

She lunged at him with her sharp claws; Daniel sidestepped out of the way and broke her elbow, rendering her arm useless. He then put his leg behind hers to push her, making her fall to the ground. He sensed Raven coming his way and waited for her patiently, anticipating her arrival at any moment to save her sister. When she had finally shown her face, Daniel dealt a blow to her face with his elbow, breaking her nose and causing her to fall to the ground.

He went on top of Penelope and, like Mortezan, began dealing blows left and right to her face.

"Please," Penelope begged. "Please stop."

The anger inside Daniel had reached its peak. He dealt one last blow to her before screaming, "Who are you to beg?"

He stood up, looking around him to make sure no one was trying to save her. With no one coming from what he could see, he helped Penelope to her feet. "Come here." He then dealt a blow to her stomach, causing her to go on her knees.

"I'm not done with you yet." Daniel once again pulled Penelope to her feet. "You shot Mary Strickland because she was willing to fight you. I had no idea who I was or what I was capable of at the time." He pushed her back down and gave her a punch to her eye.

"I was…I was only doing what…what my father wanted done." She put her hand in the air to defend herself with; Daniel, in turn, grabbed it and broke her wrist. "And now I'm doing what I should have done that day." He finally had her next to her father, who was rolling on the ground on his back. After, he would lift his arm and wait for his sword to materialize. Once it happened, he made sure Mortezan was watching. Just like he had to watch Mary die, he wanted him to cradle his daughter.

"Any last words Penelope?" Daniel asked, raising his sword above his head.

"Go ahead," he heard Mortezan say weakly. "Go ahead and kill her. If that's what will make you sleep better. Your girlfriend is still dead; your death is still certain."

Daniel's sword began to shake. He shook his head in retaliation. *No! Enough fighting with myself about what I should do!* He let out a yell and stabbed Mortezan in the chest.

Red mist began to richly come out when Daniel had taken out the sword. "You're right," he told Mortezan as the Dark Lord looked at him in shock. "Mary won't come back, but you won't either. Not for some time anyway."

Mortezan looked at Daniel as the red mist evaporated completely from his body, leaving the Dark Lord to turn into a black mist himself before disappearing for good.

He had done it. He fell to one knee, exhausted, his vision becoming blurry. He tried to stand up but couldn't. He was just too weak.

With Mortezan and his army now gone, Daniel collapsed just as the King and Queen, Anya and Balisnor were getting there, some of their soldiers present as well to serve as the royal's first line of defense.

They dragged him to the wall, Princess Anya never leaving his side.

FORTY FIVE

When Daniel had finally awoke, he found Princess Anya and Balisnor at his bedside. Anya had his hand in hers, his uncle keeping a keen eye on him.

"How are you feeling sport?" Balisnor asked, walking to the Princess' side.

"I feel like I have a headache from hell," Daniel replied. Truthfully, not only did he have a severe headache, his whole body was sore. "Did we win?"

"Oh yeah, we won. After Mortezan had disappeared, his daughters and army did likewise. One of them anyways."

"How long have I been asleep?"

Princess Anya was the one to answer. "Two weeks." She looked up at him, her eyes swollen and red, black bags under her eyes. "I haven't left your side in two weeks."

"Anya, you look like a zombie. Get some sleep."

She stood up. "Yeah, I think I will. I'll send for you when I'm awake and ready to talk." Anya was so tired, she teleported to her room, not trusting herself to walk all that way.

Balisnor took her seat. "You slipped into death a few times. Luckily, our nurse was able to bring you back. Nurse said you have a severe slash on the back of your head, but nothing to really worry about."

"That's why she looks like that."

His uncle nodded. "Afraid so. There's something you need to know though. The remaining Kingdoms are heading this way right now. They all should be here around nightfall."

"You said earlier that Mortezan and his daughters had left except one."

Balisnor sighed. "We captured Penelope. She's in our dungeon as we speak. Why didn't you kill her?"

"I didn't kill her because we need information we don't yet have."

"Worry about healing up first, and then we can worry about everything else. As soon as you're out of here, we have to get you prepared for battle."

Balisnor stood up and walked out of the hospital wing.

Daniel attempted to sit up in his bed, but an immense pain shot through his arms instantly. *The Chosen One is bedridden.* Depressed and livid at the same time, Daniel closed his eyes and drifted off once more.

FORTY SIX

*W*e underestimated the Chosen One's ability. He could hear Raven's voice in his head. *And now they have Penelope. What do we do Father?*

Mortezan had not spoken since being forced to come back to his dungeon. His eyes were the only thing one could see, and they were blazing red.

Father?

We do nothing. We wait for the right time to strike again.

What if she tells them where we are? Where you *are?*

Then so be it.

Raven looked at her father in a puzzling way. It didn't make sense that he wanted to wait again for another opportunity that would never show its face. Was he scared? Everyone, including her, had underestimated the power of Daniel's gift; but he had used it haphazardly and almost died from it. The time to strike was now. She knew it, she knew her father knew it, but he didn't want to take it. Reluctantly, she said, *Yes Father* and began to walk off.

She didn't take more than a couple of steps before her father bellowed, "Release the Assassins!

Raven bowed. "Yes, My Lord." She walked off, a smirk on her face.

FORTY SEVEN

True to Balisnor's word, they were notified of the other four Kingdoms' arrival shortly before the end of the day. Their shadows were long as the sun began to set after a long day.

"Open the gates!" Balisnor roared.

From up on top of the wall, it was a mirage of colors that were coming from the various banners spreading across the open land. From white on one side to black on the other, everywhere the King looked was like a rainbow.

The army that was positioned on the far left came through first, riding at full speed as their horses stormed to the front of the gate.

"Are you ready for this?" Queen Guinevere asked her husband.

The King laughed. "Of course not. I don't want to see this, when we just all come together to see who takes my daughter from me."

"Don't fret about it dear. She's going to stay here because Daniel is going to win."

"I hope so. The only one I truly fear is Alvaro's boy Alane. That boy scares me."

"What's the difference between you fighting for my hand and people fighting for your daughter's?"

"Times were different Guine. I loved you before this whole thing started. People are different though; if they don't win, they wage war on each other."

"It's tradition."

"It's ludicrous. I have half a mind to say its been cancelled and risk war since our men are ready for it."

Erek proceeded down the steps to greet his newcomers, pausing the conversation between them for the time being.

"If it isn't the new the new King of Varin himself!" roared a man with ocean blue armor on and sporting a round midsection. "Is the food good here or what Erek?"

They embraced like brothers before stretching their arms out to admire each other.

"The food is always good here brother. How's Mirador?"

"A disaster, but when you got a strong Queen like Daria here, it makes it worthwhile."

King Erek looked up to the top of the wall, staring at his wife. "You have no idea. Guinevere keeps me grounded in doing this every day."

"If she can put up with your anger, she must be the one for you hothead."

They both laughed. "Come inside and have your men rest up," King Erek said after he had quit laughing.

The next army that came through was adorned in silver armor with white trimming, headed by their King and Queen. The King had short wavy hair on top, his sides buzzed off. As he came nearer, Erek could see his black eyes, no color in the middle whatsoever. His wife had flowy red hair with matching red eyes; they stopped before him on top their horses, looking down at them.

King Erek cleared his throat. "Alvaro. Abelina. Thank you so much for coming."

King Alvaro put his hand up, silencing Erek. "Let's not make this any more painful than it needs to be. Where can my men sleep?"

Erek went to open his mouth in reply, but somebody from behind King Alvaro asked, "Where is the Princess?"

"She's resting," Queen Guinevere said simply.

"Too bad." The person behind the King ended up being their son. He had wholesome white eyes that matched the color of his hair as well. "I was wanting to see her."

"Alvaro, how's E-Emberlight?" Erek asked.

"Give me your strongest warrior and you'll find out," he replied as he whipped his horse to move.

I can't stand them, Guinevere said in his head as Emberlight's army filed past them. *Even if Daniel loses, as long as Alane gets in last, I'm happy.*

King Erek laughed to himself, waiting for the next King and Queen to arrive. *I feel the same way. But could you imagine Anya with him?*

Or their offspring?

Well, that image is stuck in my head. Thank you, my love.

"Greetings from Rolbrook!" the King said, leaping off his horse and hugging Erek. "How are you treating my sister?"

Rolbrook's King, Liolias, was a charismatic individual. He had a bright smile on his face; if he had to face the sun, he could have blinded Erek easily. King Liolias had wavy brown hair, brown eyes, and had a long sword on his back. His wife, Queen Amelia, was an exact reflection of her husband, but with flowing black hair and piercing silver eyes looking at Erek.

King Erek stretched out his arm and said, "As you can see, she is well. Excuse the black smoke. We had some company a few days prior to your arrival, but they've been dealt with accordingly."

Liolias nodded, stopping in his tracks. "I heard you have the Chosen One here. Is that true?"

"You need not worry about anything like that. Enjoy your time, have your men enjoy themselves. Try not to delve into anything that doesn't need no delving into."

Rolbrook's army was of pure white armor. White helmets, spears, everything. If Rolbrook's army was able to grab the sunlight in battle, their enemies would not see them coming until it was too late.

The last army that came up was headed by just a Queen. She had luscious deep red hair mixed with midnight black hair as well, black metal tips to a point covering her fingers. As she met Erek and Guinevere, she bowed her head. "Erek. Queen Guinevere. How humble it is to be here in Varin at last."

"We're glad to have you here, Queen Momonet," Erek replied. "You haven't found a suitable husband I see."

"Husbands drag you down and expect you to pop out heirs at a moment's notice. I do not have time for that now. Probably never will be, but thanks for caring."

Queen Guinevere stepped forward. "Make yourself at home Momonet. You and your soldiers. Get some rest."

As she led her soldiers away, the guard waited until the last of Momonet's army was through before closing the gate. Erek and Guinevere made their way back to the top of the wall, admiring the view.

"We get the report back tonight on what's left of Shinguard," King Erek asked. "It's still not like him to burn it down and trap us."

The Queen put her hand on her husband's shoulders. "Try not to worry about it too much my dear. He's gone, that's all that matters."

As she made her way down the steps and back toward the castle, Erek stared down at where Daniel had wounded Mortezan, making his army flee. *He knew fusing with a Hellhound was unholy, yet he did it. Why? What is wrong with you brother?*

FORTY EIGHT

Moonlight was pouring in when Daniel opened his eyes. He felt refreshed, no headache pulsing in his head, no pain radiating in his body. He moved his arms and was relieved that it didn't cost him any amount of pain. He was healed.

He sat up in bed and waited for his sight to not be as blurry. He rubbed his eyes and his vision got somewhat better; in turn, he got out of bed and stumbled. His legs gave out, making him fall to the floor. *Haven't used my legs in goodness knows how long* he thought. *I'm like a baby deer.*

When he was certain that he wouldn't fall on his face again, he slowly walked out of the wing. The hallway was empty as usual, but as he made his way to the throne room, he noticed that the guards that were usually posted at the doors were gone too. *What the hell?*

"They're all outside in the castle grounds," came a voice from the side of him.

Daniel turned around and saw a young man leaned up against the wall, cutting off pieces of an apple. He had white hair and pure white eyes. His very appearance was creepy to say the least, yet there was something about him entirely that Daniel didn't like. It could've been his aura, but his presence alone made him extremely uncomfortable.

"Who are you?" Daniel asked sternly.

The white eyed young man got off the wall and nonchalantly made his way to him, his expression blank and his eyes never leaving Daniel's. "I am someone who you don't want to get in my way of claiming that which belongs to me."

"And what is it you claim?"

"Princess Anya."

Daniel smirked, not backing down from his advances. "Sorry to tell you this, but so am I."

"What is your name?" The young man threw his apple to the side, wiping his blade on the bottom of his shirt.

"My name is Daniel. And yours?"

"Prince Alane of Emberlight. I look forward to seeing you on the battlefield." He outstretched his hand, waiting for Daniel to shake it. A year goes by fast. Hope you're ready to win your lady's hand when the time comes."

Daniel reached out and shook, never leaving Alane's eyes. "Likewise," he muttered.

With Alane gone, Daniel proceeded to go out of the castle. If what he was saying was true, Princess Anya would be down there.

Indeed they were. After a couple of minutes of remembering his way, laughter and kids screaming joyously filled his ears. He leaned over the wall and could see the King and Queen by the gate talking to what he assumed was another King and Queen.

He slowly made his way downstairs and was immediately embraced by the Princess; he had not seen her coming but could smell the sweet succulent smell of strawberry filling his nostrils.

"I've missed you," she told him as she buried her face in his chest.

"I've…missed you too," Daniel replied, struggling to breathe. "You…do you mind letting me breathe? I feel like you're about to crack my rib."

"Oh, yes sorry." She let him go and backed away a couple of meters.

Daniel, as per usual, lost his breath in seeing Anya's disappearance. She had on a long blue dress that dragged to the ground and, like the rest of the dresses that he saw her in, hugged her curves at just the right angle. On her head was a slick headband that was adorned with emerald stones around the front. "You look stunning Your Grace."

The Princess slightly bowed. "Thank you."

King Erek and Queen Guinevere appeared from between them, Daniel lowering his gaze out of respect. "Your Majesties."

King Erek put his hand on his shoulder. "It's good to see you out of bed and walking around again."

"It's a great feeling to be alive."

"Daniel," the Queen said softly, making him look up. "There is someone we'd like to introduce you to." She turned to face the King and Queen to her side. "This is King Liolias and Queen Amelia of Rolbrook."

The one known as King Liolias grabbed his hand and shook it without warning. "It is so good to meet you, Daniel! How are you enjoying Varin?"

"I love it a lot Your Majesty," Daniel replied. When the King had let go of his hand, he could feel static running up and down his arm.

"That's good! That's good!" King Liolias said exuberantly. "I look forward to seeing you in the arena soon."

"Aye!" King Erek agreed, ushering King Liolias along.

The Princess grabbed his hand and teleported quickly out of Varin, towards their usual place.

FORTY NINE

Balisnor stared at Penelope intently, looking as she didn't struggle but was limp in her shackles. He ignored the sounds of kids laughing and screaming just above him, of idle conversations between common folk. He was intent on making her talk. When she looked up, her face was bruised, her left eye sporting a large purple lump just underneath.

"For someone who likes to play games, you sure are keeping your mouth shut," Balisnor said, leaning over his chair. "Tell me what I want to know, and I won't have to inflict more pain on your body. Don't, and I'm going to have fun playing my game with you. Deal?"

When Penelope talked, her breathing was wheezy, every now and then wincing as she took a breath in. "Torture me all you want Bodyguard. I'm not telling you anything."

Balisnor got up, twisting the key in the lock before going in and closing the gate. He looked up at her, delicately putting a finger on the side of her rib to see where the pain was originating from. "The body can only take so much pain, before it gives out and shuts down." He caught her wincing as his finger lay over one of her lower ribs. "Amazing what the body can do, isn't it?"

Penelope opened her mouth slightly as Balisnor pushed against her damaged rib. It was a short stabbing pain that shot through her whole body in a matter of seconds. She tried to utter a syllable, but the pain quickly turned unbearable. Tears began to drop from her eyes. "P… ple."

Balisnor stopped. "Why did you slaughter Shinguard? What did they do to deserve such a travesty?"

"Orders. I was following orders."

"Who gave him the idea of doing something like that?"

"H-His."

Balisnor smiled. "You know, I've been dreaming of this day for a while. Does Mortezan still believe his parents, my sister, is alive?"

Penelope didn't answer. She licked her lips, trying to not let her mouth dry out. "I don't know," she said after a minute. "He closes his shell when I try to get him to answer. He might be looking through all the villages to make sure they're dead, but I don't ask. I just do what he wants me to do."

Balisnor one of his soldiers said in his head.

What? I'm busy down here. What do you want?

The officer just came back with some grave news. You aren't going to like it.

Balisnor gritted his teeth, a new fire erupting from his eyes. *I'll be there soon.* He turned back around to face Penelope. "Your games are over succubus! I swear in all of Varin, if everyone is slaughtered because of you, for every soul you reaped, I will deal that many blows!"

He exited out of the cell, locking it before running up out of the dungeon and into the morning sunlight. His fists were balled up, unconsciously not thinking about it until one of his soldiers confronted him about it. He went to his chambers, locked the door and waited for a knock from the officer in charge of conducting the report.

FIFTY

Princess Anya and Daniel were still holding hands even as their feet hit the ground and raced to the shoreline.

"Anya," Daniel called out. "Where are we going?"

They stopped at the wood line, admiring the beauty of the forest but mostly for the privacy between them and the Kingdom.

"How are your injuries holding up?" the Princess asked. "I was so worried when you didn't wake after two weeks. I knew you weren't dead, but still…" She hugged him again, but instead of tearing apart, they kept close. She ran a finger down his cheek. "Do you think we're moving too fast?" she asked softly.

Daniel smirked. "Not at all."

"Good. Because I didn't care if you were to have said yes anyway."

"Happy birthday Anya. I'm going to the human realm to get you something."

Anya scoffed. "You don't have to."

"No, but I want to."

He was happy to know that his feelings hadn't changed; in fact, they had just gotten deeper. He was determined, hellbent, on winning her hand and he wouldn't stop until he did so. His heart racing at a thousand beats a minute, he slowly began to lean in toward her while closing his eyes.

As their lips met, it felt like his brain had exploded. He lifted his hand and put it to the back of her neck, stroking her hair until he at last, reluctantly, departed. She looked at him and blushed, her cheeks so red it made him laugh.

"I love you, Daniel Gates."

"I love you, too Anya."

Hand in hand, they walked back to Varin, wanting to take their time to cherish their moments together, away from people with nobody but each other serving as company.

Later that night, as the sun set, numerous tables were lined up in the throne room, utensils and plates clinking as both royalty and peasant ate under the same roof, celebrating the Princess' birthday.

Daniel was seated next to the Princess, as per her request, and as he watched from on top so many people eating, he began to wonder… out of all the places for Mortezan to attack, why did he attack Varin?

The King on the other side of him nudged him. "That young man right there is probably going to be your most challenging adversary in the tournament. He's a fighter."

Daniel looked in the direction to where the King was pointing and found that it was Prince Alane he was referring to. "Don't worry, Your Majesty. I'll take care of him in due time."

King Erek laughed. "I know you will."

Underneath the table, Princess Anya and Daniel were holding hands in secret.

Erek stood up, taking his glass in one hand and spoon in the other to cling it, causing the glass to ring a single tune as it echoed over everyone talking and laughing, enjoying life. "Now, now," he bellowed.

The room got silent instantly, allowing the King to talk without interruption. "On behalf of all of Varin, I welcome the rest of the Four Kingdoms to my home to celebrate my daughter's sixteenth birthday."

"As per tradition, when a daughter reaches her sixteenth birthday, the rest of the Kingdoms unite to battle it out for the right to marry the host Kingdom's daughter. Considering that we only had three suitable young men, I figured to make it even. Therefore, with the blessing of my wife and I, we have decided to put a fresh face into the competition." King Erek beckoned Daniel to stand up by looking his way and nodding.

Daniel put down his glass and stood beside the King. He could feel all eyes set on him, making him suddenly sweat and make his palms sweat profusely themselves.

"Daniel Gates, Warrior of Varin, has been selected to compete for the right to win my daughter's hand in marriage. He is blessed by my wife and I and has selected by Princess Anya herself. Prince Victor, Prince Alane, and Prince Henry, here is your competition."

King Erek lifted his glass and bellowed, "May luck and fortune be on your side!"

The throne room erupted into cheers as King Erek sat down, the doors bursting open as dancers and musicians came in to liven the mood.

As they watched people dance and drink and live, King Erek tapped Daniel on the shoulder. Beckoning him to follow him, Daniel got up and walked briskly behind the King, the Princess trailing him shortly after. They walked to the chambers where the King and Queen resided, the Princess locking the door behind them, the music and laughter now mute.

A man with a gold cape stood inside waiting for them, his helmet on the table. The man was bald and looked to be bulky under all the armor, his brown eyes piercing as he held a rolled up piece of parchment.

At the sight of the royal figures, the man went down on a knee and lowered his head. "Your Majesties. Sorry to be the bearer of bad news."

The King outstretched his hand and the man gave him the parchment right away. He tore off the tie that held it together, hastily reading each line from top to bottom. There was one line, however, that Daniel could see the King's eyes slowly go over…King Erek cleared his throat and said in a shaky voice, "After careful analysis, there is reason to believe that the Dark Lord's army wiped out the entire village of Shinguard; every man, woman, and child. Shinguard, a village entrusted to Varin, has fallen."

The whole room was silent. No one moved from their places. No one talked. Daniel put his head down in shame; he knew he should've continued to stay and fight until they were all dead. Had he done it, those people might have still been alive.

Princess Anya was behind him the entire time and put her hand on his shoulder. *You can't blame yourself my love. You did all you could.*

Tears welled up in his eyes. *I should have done better. Now they're all dead.*

We would be too if you didn't turn. If you hadn't, neither of us would be here and we would be in this report.

"What do we do?" Balisnor asked. "I believe the people deserve to know."

"If we tell the people now, all we'll do is start a panic. It's better to wait until the end of the tournament," King Erek replied, putting the report down on the table and walking away.

"Your Majesty, with all due respect," Balisnor began.

"I meant what I said Bodyguard!" King Erek retaliated before slamming the door behind him.

Queen Guinevere put up a finger to shush Balisnor. "Just give him time to simmer down. Be vigilant, and double security at the gates at night."

"Yes, Your Majesty."

Daniel waited until the Queen had left before going to Balisnor. "Teach me to use my power more effectively. Please. For my sake."

"For your sake?"

"I half-ass know how to control it. The next time I face Mortezan, I might not be so lucky. Not only will it help me in the tournament, it'll also help in my future fights with him."

Balisnor thought about it for a second before saying, "Very well. Meet you at the training grounds tomorrow." Balisnor teleported out of the room, leaving the Princess and Daniel to themselves.

Raven isn't going to just roll over, Princess Anya said, coming next to him and holding his hand. *She will be back, and she's going to bring hell with her.*

Daniel held out his hand and watched as a ball of blue electricity came to life, his eyes also a dark blue to match the flames. *I'll be ready.*

EPILOGUE

She was in a war-torn castle, bits of stone missing from what used to be an extravagant building. Debris was everywhere, yet she still called this place home. How could she abandon her birthplace? She had been born here, had seen this place blossom into something unbeknownst to her at the time…until the untimely downfall. She was the rightful ruler of this place, and she would protect it with her life.

As she sat perched on the highest beam of her beloved home, she heard rustling from outside of leaves, followed by twigs breaking and voices coming from just outside the walls.

After a few minutes, two soldiers came inside and began looking around, as if searching for something.

"These spider webs are huge," she heard one person say to the other. "They're too big to be just a normal spider."

"Could be remains of the last Spider Army," the other said.

"Spider Army?"

"You really don't know your folklore, do you?" When his friend didn't speak, he went on. "They were led by a powerful Queen who trusted the wrong people and, in turn, got slaughtered by them."

"Who was their Queen?"

"Queen Islanzadi. She was thought to be the most beautiful in all the land. Now, if she's alive, there's nothing left of that pretty face."

She had heard enough. When she spoke, it was loud and clear: "Is that part of the folklore too? Because I believe you have me entirely mistaken."

They looked around, staring up at the ceiling, but it was so dark they couldn't see her even if given her vision. "W-W-Who are you? S-Show yourself!"

The woman cocked her head to the side. "Are you challenging me?"

"Show yourself!" the soldier shouted even louder than before.

"Very well." She leaped from her hiding spot and landed in front of the petrified soldiers, whose legs gave way and they crumbled to the ground. Her face was hidden, yet her eyes glowed a searing yellow. "The soldier who knows about the Spider Army, what was Queen Islanzadi known for?"

The soldier to the left was the one who answered. "She was known for her mercy."

The woman growled lowly. "What brings you here?"

"We're just scouting. We wanted to check out the ruins for signs of enemies."

"Nobody's here. Get out, and don't return."

The soldier on the left took a step closer. "A-Are you Queen Islanzadi?"

"Leave before you find out."

The soldiers took off without another warning, leaving the woman to her beloved castle once more.

"My Queen."

The woman turned to face a large tarantula looking back at her. "We need to make a comeback. We can't hide in the shadows forever."

"And do what? Get hurt again? Lose the last bit of dignity we have left?"

"Hiding in the shadows is not dignity filled Your Majesty." The tarantula's pinchers clicked together. "Our spies have reports of the Chosen One living here in Varin. If he's anything like his parents, he can make it right again. Bring respect and honor back into the Spider Army. Just send me, and I will have him here in no time."

The Queen thought about it. Was it worth it? She didn't want to send her best soldier if it meant him getting injured, or worse, killed. But what if the reports were true? Then this opportunity could be the last. She had to take the risk, and she knew this. "Go. Be swift about it as well Oman."

The tarantula bowed before running off. The Spider Army was all she had left. If the remaining members of her army were to die, then all she would do is blame herself for trusting her second in command to such a suicidal journey. Still, she had to do something to give her people hope. Now, as her stomach growled, she leapt back to her hiding place, waiting for her next prey to stumble about.

It was late at night when Raven had made her way to the local tavern. *The scent of human is beyond repulsive. I need to get this done quickly.*

She kept her head down as she went inside, past the first few sets of tables, and went to the bar. She looked up at the bartender with her purple eyes, dropping a small sack of uniki on top.

"They're in the back Princess," the bartender said, pretending to clean out a glass.

Raven got up and proceeded to the back of the bar, through the door and used her eyes to traverse the dark room that for a normal person would be difficult. She saw the four of them sitting at the table playing poker, each to themselves, concentrating.

"It's been a while since a Dark Princess has been in our presence," the one in the middle said without looking up from his cards. "To what do you owe us your presence?"

"The Chosen One is alive. We need you to kill him and anyone else who gets in your way."

All four of them laughed. *We don't work for free* they said in unison. *Give us payment or get the hell out.*

Raven unlaced the satchel strapped to her side and threw it down, a couple of uniki falling out.

The only female in the group grabbed the satchel and smiled before throwing it to her comrade, pulling back her hood and revealing pointed ears, her cold silver eyes meeting hers and never parting. "Where is this Chosen One, and how painful do you want the death?"